Where There's a Will

A Village Library Mystery, Volume 5

Elizabeth Spann Craig

Published by Elizabeth Spann Craig, 2021.

This is a work of fiction. Similarities to real people, places, or events are entirely coincidental.

WHERE THERE'S A WILL

First edition. June 15, 2021.

Copyright © 2021 Elizabeth Spann Craig.

Written by Elizabeth Spann Craig.

With thanks to John for the idea.

Chapter One

IT WAS THE KIND OF busy day at the library that made me relieved to take a lunch break. Even better was Grayson being there to share it with me. Grayson and I were embarking on a new relationship and still in the process of figuring out exactly what it all meant. One thing it definitely seemed to mean was Grayson coming over to the library at least a few times a week for conversation and lunch together.

He joined me in the sunny breakroom, full of plants, books, and magazines. Fitz, our library cat, was sprawled in a particularly large sunbeam on the floor but leaped up and looked at us with interest as we walked in. Fitz gave every appearance of absolutely adoring Grayson Phillips. He bumped his head lovingly against Grayson's extended hand and closed his eyes happily as Grayson tickled him gently under his furry chin.

I said, "Whatever food you've brought smells amazing. Did you grab takeout from somewhere?" Whitby, however, was such a small town that my mind boggled trying to figure out what place might have produced such a tantalizing aroma.

Grayson grinned at me, his blue eyes crinkling. "Nope. This is actually something I cooked this morning especially for our lunch today."

"Now you've piqued my curiosity. And maybe made me a little envious. My cooking has been pretty pedestrian lately. Okay, it's *always* been pedestrian. What have you made?"

He carefully removed two bone china plates from the bag he carried them in and held one out with a flourish. "Pasta with shrimp and bechamel sauce."

My stomach growled on cue. "Wow. And you made this today? Before you went to work? How early did you get up this morning?"

Grayson was carefully setting the laminated breakroom table with a cheerful tablecloth, cloth napkins, and silverware. "Oh, I don't know. Five o'clock? Something like that? It wasn't a big deal, really—you know how quickly shrimp cooks."

I figured I probably would if I ever cooked it. My own kitchen adventures seemed to revolve around rice and whatever was leftover in my fridge to go along with it. There was also the fact that I had budget issues that came into play when I made food choices at the grocery store. I loved being a librarian, but I wasn't exactly becoming King Midas being one. "Well, this is a real treat. Thanks so much."

He gave me a shy smile and then reached over and hugged me tightly. I hugged back, feeling the muscles in his arms from all his outside activities when he *wasn't* at his newspaper job. Then he pulled away. "I warmed up the plates at the office, but they could probably use a few seconds more in the microwave."

While he was doing that, I poured us both some ice waters from the pitcher in the fridge and gave Fitz another rub.

"No shrimp for you, buddy," Grayson said regretfully as he glanced over to watch us. "I can see your little nose is really twitching. But I did bring a few cat treats with me."

"Now you're spoiling both of us." I chuckled as I said it, though. I hadn't been spoiled much in life and it was sort of a nice change of pace.

We delved enthusiastically into the food and it tasted just as good as it smelled. The flavors mingled perfectly together.

"The only thing lacking is a glass of wine," said Grayson. "But, hey, it's the middle of the workday."

"Sadly, I'm probably going to feel like a big nap, even *without* a midday glass of wine. Once this pasta hits my tummy, I'm going to need to make sure I have a cup of coffee with me for a while."

"I'll make some fresh coffee for you," said Grayson.

I watched him as he dumped out the stale coffee and made a new pot. My feelings grew stronger for him every day, especially as he consistently performed small kindnesses. He turned around, feeling my eyes on him, and gave his quirky smile.

"How are things going with the construction?" He sat back down with me as the coffee percolated and Fitz hopped in his lap, regarding him thoughtfully.

I groaned. The library was undergoing some much-needed renovation work, but it was a very noisy process. The construction noises were annoying the patrons who'd come over to get some studying or work done. Plus, construction vehicles were impacting available parking, too.

"Well, the patrons are cranky and I can't really blame them. I think the noise has run quite a few of them off. But the library is going to be so much better when the work is done."

"I bet Fitz isn't crazy about the construction, either," said Grayson. He reached into his pocket and pulled out a couple of treats. The cat gave him an affectionate look. I could swear Fitz was smiling.

"You've got that right. His tail swishes whenever he hears a drill. Or hammering. Which is pretty much all day. But he really likes the guys who are *doing* the construction. In fact, they've been giving him cat treats and playing with him with one of his cat toys."

We washed off our empty plates and walked out of the breakroom with Fitz trailing behind us. His ears went back at the sound of the drill and he bounced off to find a patron's lap or a sunbeam to comfort him as the construction went on.

"Which one is the guy in charge of the work?" asked Grayson in a low voice. "From what you've said, he sounds like an interesting person to know."

I gestured to a distinguished-looking man in his mid-fifties with wavy white hair. "His name is Cornelius Butler. I've spent some time talking with him and he's a really interesting guy. He went to Clemson for engineering, was a project manager for big projects, and he's now working as a real estate investor and builder. He owns the construction firm that's doing the work. Like I mentioned before, he's doing the work pro-bono and so he's Wilson's new best friend."

Wilson was my library director and always had an eye out for the chance to butter up donors or trustees. And Cornelius definitely deserved buttering up. What he was doing was really going to improve the library building—once the construction was finally done. The work entailed everything from carpet installation to new light fixtures, upgraded restrooms to an expanded children's department that makes better use of the space.

"What's Cornelius like?" asked Grayson curiously.

I smiled at him. "Are you thinking about doing a profile on him in the newspaper?" Grayson had been running a series of profiles of prominent local citizens in the paper and it had proven a popular feature with folks in the town. And, of course, the featured citizen absolutely loved it.

"Maybe so. He's certainly worthy of it. And it serves several good purposes when I run one of those articles: it sells papers, helps me get to know an influential resident, and makes the profiled person happy. I haven't focused on anyone in the construction industry yet, so it makes sense."

"I can introduce you to him, if you like," I said. "The library is pretty quiet right now."

But Cornelius was already taking care of that, himself. He walked over with a twinkle in his eyes and a hand outstretched. "Cornelius Butler," he said, giving Grayson a firm handshake.

Grayson introduced himself, but before he could say anything else, Cornelius said, "Ah! Our local newspaper editor. It's a pleasure to meet you. I've been wanting to email you to congratulate you on the recent series you did on unusual local history."

Grayson looked as if the pleasure was all his. I had the feeling that he wasn't used to having his name recognized during an introduction. "Good to meet you, too and thanks for reading the series. I was just speaking with Ann about the project here. This is a fantastic thing you're doing for the library."

Cornelius modestly shook his head. "For all the hours of pleasure the library has afforded me over the years, believe me, it's the very least I can do. But tell me how things are going over at the newspaper. I know it hasn't been a good time for print."

This was one of Grayson's most-favorite subjects, but he managed to refrain from launching into his full spiel, instead saying, "Actually, the paper is doing pretty well . . . probably because it's one of the few sources of real local information. Of course, we're not just running printed papers—our digital subscriptions are up, too. Long-term, that might be the best way for the paper to really remain viable because it lowers our overall costs." He paused and then chuckled. "Sorry—you can tell this is one of my favorite topics."

But Cornelius didn't have that glazed look on his face that I'd seen on others' faces when Grayson started talking publishing. He'd leaned in and seemed to be hanging on his every word. He had a habit of doing this to everyone and seemed to use conversations with people as a way to increase his own knowledge in a variety of different fields. "No, no worries. That's actually really interesting. I've been toying with the idea of doing some advertising and would love to speak with you about that."

His words were music to Grayson's ears. "Absolutely. We have an advertising representative that I can get you in touch with."

"Could I just speak with you instead?" asked Cornelius in the voice of a man who never really had his requests denied.

"Most definitely," said Grayson. He wouldn't jeopardize a sale, even if his handling advertising wasn't totally protocol. "You can call me at any time."

Cornelius turned his head sharply and looked behind him, squinting at something that was taking place across the room.

"Nate!" he bellowed.

Nate, a tall, lean man about thirty years old with an open face, froze.

"Stop what you're doing right now!" Cornelius strode across the library. He briefly turned around to say, "Nice to meet you," to Grayson before immediately addressing whatever horrible thing Nate had done with the construction work. "Nate! Remember: do your best and caulk the rest."

"Poor guy," said Grayson, shaking his head. "Looks like he's really messed something up."

I made a face and said in a low voice, "It's always like that. I'm never sure exactly what he's doing wrong, but he seems to be making a real hash of it, whatever he's doing."

Grayson frowned. "A professional guy like that? It's hard to believe he wouldn't have the very best people on his team."

"Oh, believe me, he does. He has a fleet of them. They're quiet—well, aside from all the construction noise—and totally focused on what they're doing. It's been very impressive."

"So what's the deal with Nate?" asked Grayson.

"The deal with Nate is that he's Cornelius's nephew, apparently." I gave Grayson a wry smile.

"Ahh. That makes a lot more sense. I'm guessing he's new to the construction industry?" Grayson started walking to the door and I kept up with him.

"That's what Cornelius told me. He's originally from another state but lost his job there and came here to North Carolina to find one. His uncle has taken him on as an apprentice but it wasn't what he was doing previously. I think it's been quite an adjustment."

Grayson winced as Cornelius continued reminding Nate how he'd messed up. "Maybe he needs to think about another line of work. Or maybe he should take a class or something." He glanced at his watch and said, "Better run. I've got someone to interview in a few minutes."

I reached out and squeezed his hand. "Thanks for lunch."

He gave me a warm smile and squeezed my hand back. "See you later."

I walked behind the circulation desk and Fitz pounced up to join me. I rubbed him a few times and spoke to him soothingly as the sound of the drills started up again. A man with black hair and heavy eyebrows that were furrowed in a frown came in. He hesitantly walked into the library, spotted the construction and stopped, uncertainly.

I called out, "Hi there. Can I help you with anything?"

He gave me a startled look and scurried back out of the building.

I was staring after him, frowning, when I heard a teasing voice from my left.

"Scaring patrons away now, Ann?"

I turned and smiled at my coworker, Luna. She was one of those people who always *did* make you smile . . . usually in a peppy, happy mood that was contagious to be around. She was also cheerful to look at with her Doc Martin shoes, long multi-colored tunic, and purple-streaked hair. "Apparently, I am," I said dryly.

"It was probably the unholy racket coming from the construction that frightened him away. It sure has unnerved poor Fitz and he's such a laid-back boy. If I'd come into the library to get some work done or to study then I'd definitely be backing right back out again, too. It's too loud to even hear yourself think," said Luna. Then she gave me a knowing smile. "How was lunch with Grayson? Great, as always?"

"Very nice! A little on the noisy side, of course, with the drill work going on, but still good. He brought me a shrimp pasta he'd cooked this morning and it was amazing."

"Of course it was!" Luna rolled her eyes teasingly. "Everything he does is amazing."

A mother with a little boy in tow walked up to ask Luna if she had any recommendations for good picture books and Luna happily led them to the children's section, prattling off her favorites as she went.

I worked a bit on a research question a patron had given me yesterday to learn more about a health condition her husband had. After a while, the doors opened again and an older lady timidly came in wearing a fluffy cardigan sweater, her gaze darting around the library. When she spotted Fitz with me, she started to smile.

"Hi, Olivia," I said gently. She was so hesitant that I felt she needed some encouragement. I knew she loved cats and had quite a few of them at her house. I also knew she was Cornelius Butler's sister. "Your brother is right over there—did you want to see him?"

Olivia immediately looked alarmed. "Oh no. No, I don't need to talk with him. I'm just here to love on Fitz and pick up my books."

Fitz was, as always, happy to be the recipient of some love. He bumped his head against Olivia's outstretched hand and gazed affectionately at her. She crooned to him. "What a beautiful boy you are! And so good, too. You remind me of my Humphrey Bogart."

"Is Humphrey an orange and white cat, too?" I asked.

She nodded, eyes twinkling. "He's one of the best lap cats I have, but don't tell the others. I just love when I sit and read and he's curled up in my lap."

Every time I saw Olivia, I wondered if she'd consider going to one of the library's book clubs. She was a big reader and seemed to enjoy talking about books with me. And she spent a lot of time . . . too much time? . . . at home with her collection of cats.

"I was thinking you might enjoy our book club, Olivia—the one we host at the library here. We're about to have a meeting to discuss a book you recommended to me earlier. *Arabella.*"

Olivia beamed. "Oh, that's a wonderful book. Georgette Heyer is simply marvelous. Goodness, I must have read that book twenty times."

"Well, I enjoyed it too after you told me about it. I needed to read some more Regency books and *Arabella* fit the bill. If you're interested, just drop in with us." I gave her the date and time. "After all, you know the book a lot better than we do."

Olivia hesitated and then smiled. "I'll see what I can do. I would really like hearing what other people think about it." She paused. "Do you have any other recommendations for Regencies? I mean, that some of your patrons have enjoyed?"

I took her back in the stacks to Sherry Lynn Ferguson's *Lord Sidley's Last Season*, which Olivia immediately checked out at the circulation desk.

I was about to take my afternoon break when there was another arrival at the library. I grinned as Connor, Wilson's nephew and a former classmate and boyfriend of mine, came in. He was cocky as ever in his scrubs, striding up to the circulation desk.

"What brings you here today?" I asked teasingly. "Surely not literature."

Connor put his hand to his heart. "You wound me, Ann! You know I love to read. I've just found that I'm in a particular period of my life where I can't read as much as I'd like."

"You're here to see Wilson, then," I smiled. "He's in his office. I'm getting ready to take my break."

"Well, I'm here to see you, too. I was hoping you could give me some advice."

I raised my eyebrows. "Lovelorn again, are you?"

"I'll tell you all about it in the breakroom."

I rolled my eyes. "So now you're commandeering my break."

"Oh, come on, Ann. You know you're my only friend here in this town. Help a guy out?" His eyes were pleading.

I sighed. "Okay. Just tap on the door and I'll let you in. I'm guessing you're wanting to say hi to Wilson first?"

He nodded, looking pleased. "See you in a few."

Chapter Two

FITZ FOLLOWED ME INTO the breakroom and padded right to a sunbeam that came through the big window in there. I grabbed a granola bar and poured myself a cup of coffee to ensure I could make it through the rest of the day with as much energy as I needed.

It wasn't long before Connor tapped on the door. Fitz watched with interest from his sunbeam as I walked over and opened the door to let him in. Seeing Connor, he trotted over and wound himself through his legs, purring loudly.

"See? I'm likeable," said Connor, reaching down to pick up the cat and sit in one of the chairs with him.

I raised my eyebrows. "Is that in question?" Connor *was* a likeable guy. He was an extrovert, he was funny. He was interesting, too, with lots of stories from his work in emergency medicine. He could definitely carry a conversation. But he hadn't been good relationship material since he was, among other things, a little too self-focused.

Connor gave me a glum look. "Apparently. I could use some dating advice."

"Dating advice from *me*?"

Connor grinned at me. "Is that totally out of the question?"

"Well, it's hardly my area of expertise, after all. If you'd asked me to help you find resources to research your family tree or wanted some tips for using Excel spreadsheets, *those* are things that I could better help you with." I did have a boyfriend now. But my barren wasteland of a dating life previous to Grayson didn't bear reflecting on.

"But you're a woman."

"That we can agree on. Although I don't know if it makes me specially qualified to advise you on whatever mess you've gotten yourself into," I said.

Connor said, "So here's the thing. I really like this woman, Victoria."

I frown. "Hm. Victoria. I don't think I know any Victorias. And this isn't such a big town."

"She doesn't actually live here in Whitby . . . she's in Iva. I met her at work."

My frown deepened. "Well, that's even *more* of a problem, isn't it? Aren't there ethical considerations there? Aren't workplace romances frowned upon?"

Connor sighed. "The main problem is that it *isn't* a workplace romance. I'd just like for it to be."

"Is she just not interested?" I suggested.

Connor gave me an indignant look. "Of *course* she's interested. Why wouldn't she be?"

I said mildly, "Maybe you're not her type."

This had clearly not occurred to Connor and he frowned, his brows knitting together. "I'm not sure that's the problem."

"Have you asked her out yet? For a coffee or something?"

"I asked her out to dinner," said Connor with a shrug.

I had some experience with Connor asking someone out for dinner since I'd dated him briefly. I remembered in particular a very nice evening planned in a nearby town. But he'd made it into something of an event with us dressing up, etc. I had the feeling he might be coming on a little strong to Victoria.

"Why don't you dial it back a notch? Maybe you could just casually ask her if she'd like to meet up for a coffee after work. Don't make it be a big deal . . . just go in your scrubs. Then try and focus on her and find out what she's interested in." I added the last since it sometimes happened that Connor focused a little too much on himself.

Connor nodded slowly and then gave me a grin. "See? You are good at this."

I looked at my watch. "And now my coffee break is over, so I better get back to it."

We left the breakroom together, nearly colliding with Wilson, who was on his way in. His brows furrowed as he spotted Connor, who gave him a pat on the back. "See you soon, Wilson."

Wilson grunted in reply and gave me an inscrutable look before heading quickly into the breakroom.

"Friendly, isn't he?" said Connor cheerfully. "See you soon, Ann."

I went back to the desk and started creating graphics for the library's social media to advertise different upcoming events. I also took a couple of surreptitious pictures of Fitz because he was lying on his back with his front paws crossed and looking blissful. I knew if he saw me looking at him that he'd immediately leap up and interact with me.

I was only able to take a couple of pictures when someone else disturbed Fitz's happy slumber. Cornelius walked up and Fitz quickly greeted him with his rattling purr and a mew. Cornelius was clearly a cat person, which was another reason to like him. He loved on Fitz for a couple of minutes, crooning to him while Fitz lapped it up.

Cornelius said in a rueful tone, "I think I messed up your photo opp, Ann. You were taking some pictures of Fitz, weren't you?"

I laughed it off. "No problem. When you've got a subject as cute as Fitz is, there are plenty of opportunities for pictures. You've probably seen that Fitz helps us with our social media here at the library. Our posts get a lot more engagement when he's featured in them."

"I can imagine." Cornelius chuckled. He gave me a teasing look. "I liked your young man. Grayson, wasn't it?"

I felt myself blushing a little. "I think he liked you, too. Sounds like you might have an interview with the paper in your future."

"Works for me. I can always use the publicity for my firm." He gave Fitz a final rub and then said, "I'm about to head out for the day. I think I'm getting a little too annoyed with my crew and I need to just remove myself for a while."

It had sounded to me like it was just his nephew taking the heat, but I nodded in understanding.

He said, "Before I left, I wanted to ask you if the library was accepting donations. For books, I mean. I just moved into my new place on the lake and I realized during the move that I have far too many books. If I had enough bookcases to hold them all, I'd be blocking the view from all the huge windows I installed to see the lake and mountains."

"The Friends of the Library would love the books for their book sale and all the profits go to help the library purchase materials," I said quickly. "That would be fantastic."

"The only problem with books is the weight of them. And there are quite a few of them to move."

I took this as a request. And, with a person like Cornelius Butler, you definitely did whatever he requested.

"Oh, Wilson and I can help with that. I'd imagine you'd like the books out of the way as quickly as possible, right? I'm sure you don't want boxes of books lying around." I included Wilson in the plan because I knew he always looked forward to opportunities to network.

He looked relieved and gave me the grin that had probably helped get him his way on numerous occasions. "That would be fantastic, Ann. When do you think you might make it over?"

"Whenever is the best time for you. I know you're usually over here at the library first thing in the morning—if it worked for you, Wilson and I could swing by your house tomorrow morning before we head in to work."

Cornelius said, "That would be perfect. That way, we get them out early." He grinned again. "I love being productive early in the day. And I have an elevator, which will help with getting the books out of the house."

I must have looked surprised at the mention of the elevator because Cornelius laughed. "It's a tall house. I wanted the best views and I needed to go up to get them. I could have built a home in the mountains and gotten the view that way, but I really liked the idea of a house on the lake. The only problem was hauling groceries and packages up the stairs. The elevator works great for that." He paused and looked past me at something his nephew was doing in the background. He shook his head, wincing. "Sorry. I shouldn't let it get to me. Nate is trying to learn the business, but he's having a tough time. Seeing him make mistakes or bumble around is just completely exhausting for me."

I nodded. "I'm sure it's hard to have an apprentice." He seemed like the kind of guy who was used to forging out on his own, not delegating. And he definitely didn't seem much like a teacher to me, either. He didn't appear to have the patience for it. And he was clearly something of a perfectionist, too, from what I'd been able to witness.

Cornelius brushed off my sympathy. "Oh, I'll be fine. It's just that my family, as a whole, seems to wear me out. Do you find that to be true?"

I said, somewhat apologetically, that I didn't have a family.

Cornelius looked at me sadly. "I'm so sorry. I should feel fortunate for the family I do have. I can't imagine not having one at all."

There was a crash in the background and Cornelius closed his eyes briefly. "I should go ahead and head out. I'll see you and Wilson tomorrow morning."

After he walked out, Wilson came up to the desk. He peered out the door as Cornelius climbed into an SUV. "He's leaving for the day?"

"Yes. And I hope it's all right with you, but I volunteered both of us for picking up his book donations at Cornelius's house tomorrow morning before work."

"Of *course* that's okay. Cornelius has been wonderful to the library. Whatever makes him happy is fine with me." He cleared his throat and looked uncomfortable. I had a feeling that I knew what he was about to say next.

Sure enough, with a bit of hemming and hawing, he said, "I saw Connor was hanging out with you in the breakroom. I do hope my nephew was behaving himself."

I hid a smile. Wilson was always looking after me. Well, except when he was dumping more work on my desk, which he frequently did. "Connor was just wanting to ask my opinion about something."

Wilson looked doubtful and I elaborated, "He's interested in dating someone and wanted my advice on how to approach it."

Wilson looked surprised. "And he was going to follow your advice?"

I laughed. "That remains to be seen. You know how Connor is."

"I certainly do. Which is precisely why I like the fact that you're seeing Grayson, instead." His voice was gruff. He gave a big cough and said, "Anyway, I'll see you in a bit. I've got quite a few things on my to do list today, I'm afraid." He hurried off.

The next morning, I was awake before the alarm went off. I'd been doing that a lot, just sort of waking up, and looking at the clock to see it was five minutes before the time the alarm was set for. I'd spend those five minutes slowly waking up and thinking about what my day was going to look like.

For a planner like me, library life wasn't *always* the most predictable thing in the world. There were definitely things already on the schedule that I knew about . . . storytimes, book club meetings, technology classes, film club, crafts, etc. But there were also a lot of things that would unexpectedly come up during the course of the day. When I started working as a librarian, I thought those kinds of surprises would possibly unsettle me a little bit. Instead, I was happy to discover that they often provided the highlights of my day—the times when I foraged a connection to one of our younger patrons or had somebody tell me that they loved the last book I'd recommended for them and ask if I could find something else for them to read.

This morning, I knew my plan started with Cornelius Butler and Wilson. So instead of lying around and doing much thinking about the upcoming day, I decided to hop out of bed and get started with it. Fitz, still lying on a blanket on my bed, opened his eyes just a crack and then closed them again. Apparently, getting up early wasn't exactly on his list of things to do for the day.

I got showered and dressed and then fixed myself a bigger-than-usual breakfast. Actually, it was more like I was extremely absentminded when I cracked the eggs into the frying pan not bothering to count the number that were going in there. There was a light tap on my kitchen door and I startled before smiling as I saw Grayson.

"Hey there you," I said softly, opening the door.

Grayson gave me a kiss, his lips gently grazing mine. "Looks like I have perfect timing."

"Oh, please take an egg. Or even two. I lost count when I was making them this morning. Or maybe I thought Fitz was going to want a plate."

"Are you sure? I was just kidding. I did have a bite to eat at home before I came over."

I gave him a look. I knew what usually constituted breakfast over at Grayson's house. He was an excellent cook, as he'd demonstrated once again yesterday at lunch, but he tended to get distracted by his phone while making breakfast. "Let me guess. Toast? Well-done? Toast flambé"?"

He grinned at me. "It *was* slightly charred, now that you mention it."

Grayson helped himself to an egg and a slice of non-burned toast and sat down at my small kitchen table with me. We ate quietly for a few moments and I realized how natural it felt to have him there. The sunlight was starting to stream through the kitchen door and Fitz moved sleepily from my bedroom and curled up in a patch on the floor, happily stretching. It was quiet and peaceful in the room at the start of the day. I smiled over at Grayson.

"What's your day look like?" he asked. I loved the way he asked questions—not offhandedly or as if it was just small talk, but as if he really wanted to know the answer. Maybe that was his own innate curiosity, the reporter in him.

"I was trying to figure that out myself when I was in the shower," I said with a laugh. "I've kind of given up on having a total handle on my days at the library because there are always so many surprises that pop up along the way. But there are some things I know I'm doing today. One of them is heading over to Cornelius's house with Wilson before going to the library. He has some books to donate that he no longer has room for."

"Does he live in a small place?" asked Grayson with a furrow creasing his brow as if he couldn't really square that with the man he'd met the day before at the library.

"No, I think it's just the opposite. An elevator was mentioned, so that tells me it's probably pretty big. He decided bookshelves would obscure the views he's paying so much for."

Grayson nodded, but glanced around my cottage. There were bookshelves lining every wall and books were stacked against a couple of walls in what I hoped was an artful way. I laughed ruefully. "Yeah, that wouldn't happen here. No views, just books."

"Books *are* the view here. And you know it's the same at my place, too. I do have a lot of digital books but I can't seem to get rid of the print books I have. I like going back and flipping through them or having a total re-read."

This was something else I liked about Grayson. Books were friends of his. Something else we had in common.

There was a brisk tap at the door, which startled me. I was wondering if I'd lost track of time and if Wilson was already there to pick me up.

Grayson already had an impish grin on his face. "Zelda," he murmured.

I groaned as I walked over to open the door. Zelda Smith was our homeowner association president. For a long time, she'd endlessly harassed me to join the board. I was delighted that she seemed to have given up on that pursuit since she'd coaxed Grayson to join, instead.

"Can I help you, Zelda?" I asked politely with my best smile.

Zelda peered around me and into the kitchen. Grayson gave her a cheery wave. Zelda sniffed in disapproval at what our early breakfast might possibly signify.

"It's your grass," said Zelda.

I nodded. I should have known her visit might pertain to the length of my grass. I totally agreed that I needed to mow. It had rained the last two times I'd had a day off from work, and consequently, my yard was starting to resemble a prairie. "Sorry about that. I'm going to get to it just as soon as I can. The rain came at inopportune times." I chuckled.

Zelda did not give a chuckle in return. She simply sniffed again. "Thank you, Ann. I appreciate your prompt attention." She quirked an eyebrow at Grayson and stiffly took her leave.

"Looks like I have an extra assignment." I gave Grayson a weary smile.

"Hey, I can take care of your grass for you. It won't take me but a minute."

I shook my head firmly. "Nope. I appreciate it, but it's my responsibility. And honestly, I don't mind handling it. I like doing yard work." I looked regretfully at the clock. "Unfortunately, I'd better get ready for when Wilson picks me up."

Grayson looked a little wistful. "Got it."

"I'm sorry," I said. I meant it—aside from our breakroom lunch yesterday, it seemed like he and I were having a tough time finding a few moments to spend together. And often the trouble seemed to be on my end.

Grayson gave me a small smile. "Believe me, I know how busy you are over at the library. It's always busy whenever I'm over there. I just wish we could spend more time together, that's all."

I said quickly, "Oh, me too. But I know it won't always be like this. Sometimes life is crazier than other times."

But Grayson didn't look so certain. And, honestly, he was right. The library consumed as much time as I let it. I was there early and sometimes I left late. During the day, I could be really slammed with patron after patron asking everything from how to get homework help to how to get started researching their family tree.

Grayson added, "It's not like I'm not busy at the paper. I don't mean to say it's all on your side. But I guess my schedule is a little more flexible."

I chuckled. "Well, you're able to leave your office during the day, which is a big difference, I guess. But you make a good point. I'm going to be on the lookout for some extra pockets of time. Or try and make some."

He gave me a tight hug and a kiss that made my head spin before he headed out the door.

Chapter Three

MINUTES LATER, I GOT a text from Wilson that he was outside. I hopped in the car and said, "Just making sure—you're dropping me back home after we pick up the books, right? Because I don't have Fitz with me and you know how there are people who come to the library *just* to spend time with Fitz."

Wilson chuckled. "Believe me, I wouldn't dream of leaving Fitz at your house for the day. No, I'll drop you by here and then maybe when you get to the library, you can help me unload the books. We should still have plenty of time before the library opens.

He set off toward the lake, classical music playing on his radio from the local college's classical radio station.

I said, "I didn't really know Cornelius before this project started, even though I saw him from time to time checking out books. I got the impression you know him better than that though. Is that right?"

Wilson said, "Oh, I know him fairly well, I suppose. He's been at board-related events and has come to some library fundraisers. We've had lunch together from time to time. Networking, you know."

I hid a smile at his tone. Although Wilson fervently believed in being very good to people who were generous to the library, I'd gotten the feeling that networking was the toughest part of his job and the one he looked least forward to. But he did a great job at it. He was a little stiff, a little formal, but he was real. There was nothing false about Wilson. And he tried very hard.

"Have you been to his house before?" I asked. "The new one, I mean. Cornelius was talking about it a little and I was curious."

"He took me by when it was under construction," said Wilson. "It was far from being done, but I was able to get a good idea of what it was going to end up looking like. What did he say to you about it?"

"Not a lot, but I got the impression it's very large."

"It is. Mostly, it's tall. Cornelius mentioned that he wanted to have a good vantage point to see both the mountains and the lake. And there are plenty of windows to do that. Floor to ceiling windows."

"Sounds like a fantastic view," I said.

We chatted quietly for a few minutes while the classical music played in the background and Wilson sipped his coffee from a travel mug every once in a while. After a bit, we reached the house. It was huge, as I'd suspected, but it also strangely seemed to blend in well with the neighborhood around it. He'd kept a lot of the big trees surrounding the back and sides of the house, leaving the front treeless for the view. Cornelius's Cadillac was parked in the driveway and we pulled up next to it.

Wilson and I got out of the car and Wilson opened up his trunk. "I did think to bring some boxes. I wasn't sure how many books he was talking about."

"He didn't really give me much of an idea either, although it sounded like a good many." He and I divided up the boxes between us and headed toward the house. I was glad to see they were old produce boxes from the grocery store because they had handles on both sides and wouldn't get loaded up so high that the boxes couldn't be easily lifted.

We set the boxes at the back door and Wilson rang the doorbell. We waited for a minute and then frowned at each other.

"Well, it's a big house," I said. "It probably takes him a while to get downstairs."

"I think he uses an elevator," said Wilson, brow furrowed.

"Maybe he's running the water inside and couldn't hear us," I suggested.

Wilson rang the bell again and we waited.

"This is most unlike Cornelius." Wilson pulled his cell phone out of his pocket. "I'll see if I can reach him."

But the phone rang and rang until his voicemail picked up.

"Maybe he's had a fall. Or a health emergency of some kind. Maybe we should see if we can get inside," I suggested.

I knew the idea would make Wilson cringe and I did see him wince. The last thing he'd want to do is invade Cornelius's privacy by coming inside. But he did also want to make sure we couldn't be of assistance somehow.

"How about if you keep trying to reach him by calling and ringing the bell and I'll check to see if any of the entrances are unlocked," I said.

Wilson considered this before giving a curt nod and putting his finger to the doorbell again, followed by knocking at the door.

The door coming off the driveway was locked. I walked around the side of the house and tried a door I saw there—locked. Then I walked around back to the front of the house that faced the lake and the mountains, noticing some landscaping that appeared to be in progress, but no sign of Cornelius. I went up the stairs and up to the deck that had sliding glass doors. They were unlocked.

I called out to Wilson to join me and then said, "Cornelius? It's Ann. Wilson and I are here to pick up the books."

I couldn't hear anything—not Cornelius and not any water running or music or anything else that would make it hard for him to hear me. I hesitated and then called Cornelius again.

By now, Wilson had joined me, his features tense. "Nothing?" he asked.

I shook my head. "Shouldn't we go inside and check on him? You said that being late for a meeting would be out of character for him, right?"

Wilson nodded.

We set down the boxes we'd brought. Then I took a deep breath and stepped into the house. Although he'd sounded as if he was still working on moving in, the house looked completely furnished and completed to me. Wilson and I continued calling for Cornelius while turning on lights and looking through the different rooms of the huge house. All we came across were some boxes stacked neatly against a wall.

Wilson peered at them through his glasses. "Labeled for the library," he said gruffly.

"Maybe we should call Burton."

Wilson looked uneasy. "Let's keep trying to find Cornelius for a couple of minutes first. I don't think he'd appreciate having the police show up if he simply overslept."

I nodded but had the feeling something was wrong. Cornelius didn't sound like the kind of guy to oversleep. In fact, from what I'd seen at the library every morning, he showed every indication of being a morning person.

Finally, we'd covered the entire house. Wilson and I looked at each other.

"He's not here," I said.

Wilson shook his head. "He's got to be. His car is outside. I don't think he'd have gone for a walk and missed meeting up with us."

I glanced over at the elevator. We'd been using the stairs. "We haven't checked the elevator," I said slowly.

Wilson frowned. "I suppose he could have experienced a medical event there."

I walked over and pressed the button for the elevator. The doors opened—but the elevator wasn't there.

I looked over at Wilson in horror and his face turned pale. We perched on the edge and looked down through the opening to see Cornelius—splayed on the top of the elevator at the bottom of the shaft.

Chapter Four

WE CALLED BURTON IMMEDIATELY. Wilson walked over to perch gingerly in one of Cornelius's fine leather armchairs.

"Are you all right?" I asked him. "Want me to get you some water or something?"

He shook his head. "I'll be fine," he said gruffly. He paused. "Should we go outside? Are we perhaps trampling on evidence?"

"You think it was foul play then?"

He shrugged helplessly. "I don't know. It's just that Cornelius is an engineer. I can't imagine an accident occurring with his elevator like this. It seems as if he'd have made sure it was in excellent working order."

He stood up and we carefully left the way we came in, picking up our empty boxes, and waiting for Burton by Wilson's car.

Burton arrived within minutes, along with an ambulance. I very much doubted there was anything the ambulance could do, having taken a look at Cornelius, but I was glad they were there. We pointed them inside and they hurried in.

After some time while Wilson paced and I shifted from foot to foot, other police cars pulled up, apparently from the state police. Then Burton came back out to join us. His face was grim.

Wilson asked nervously, "So was it an accident? Some sort of design problem with the elevator?"

Burton shook his head. "That looks pretty unlikely. There's a safety mechanism on the elevator that wouldn't have allowed the doors to open if the elevator was being held on the bottom floor. But that lock had been taken off, which would have to have been deliberate unless Cornelius did it himself. Did either of you get the feeling that he might want to harm himself in any way?"

I shook my head and Wilson said, "On the contrary. Cornelius was looking forward to spending time here in his new house and had just moved in. He'd also made plans with Ann and me to pick up some books we saw boxed up in the house to get them out of his way."

"And you were coming by here to do that this morning, obviously."

Wilson nodded. "Ann arranged with him to come by before we went to the library." He looked at his watch and winced slightly. Always a stickler for punctuality, I guessed he was starting to feel very anxious about getting over to the library to open up.

Burton jotted down a couple of notes. "It sure doesn't sound as if he was planning to die this morning."

An old sedan with the paint chipping off it pulled up and a man with black hair and thick eyebrows peered out of the window at the assorted police vehicles.

I said quickly, "I saw this guy at the library yesterday. He came in, looked around for a second, then took off again."

Burton started walking toward the car. "That's quite a coincidence."

The man's eyes widened and he put the car in gear and started driving off. But Burton stepped quickly in front of the car and held his hand up. "Stop!"

The man quickly did and then sat, slumping a bit behind the wheel.

"Come on out, please," said Burton in a commanding voice.

Wilson looked at his watch again nervously and said to me, "I'm going to call Luna and ask her to open up for us today. Can you just wait here for a few? I also need to try to call in someone else to help out since we're both here."

I nodded and Wilson stepped away to make his phone calls.

Burton gestured toward me and I stepped closer to him and the man, who had wiry arms but a bit of a beer belly.

"Ann, you said you spotted this gentleman at the library yesterday, right?"

I sighed a little to myself. Being at the library wasn't a crime, but it was kind of odd that the same man would be both places, especially with foul play suspected. "That's right. He looked as if he might be looking for someone."

The man's thick eyebrows beetled as he stared at me. "It's no crime to look for somebody." His voice was defensive.

Burton said in a gentler tone, "Of course it's not. We're just trying to get a fuller picture of what's going on here. Maybe you can help fill us in. First off, what's your name?"

"Samson Green," muttered the man.

Burton jotted it down in his notebook. "All right. Mr. Green, can you tell me what business you had with Cornelius Butler?"

Samson's expression was sullen. "Nothing much. Just wanted to talk to him and he wasn't answering my calls or texts so I tried to find him in person."

"It sounds like you're being pretty persistent. Whatever business it was must have been important to you."

Samson shrugged a thin shoulder. "It was personal."

Burton waited. This was a technique I'd seen him use before, to his advantage. He acted as if he had all the time in the day to ask another question, leaving a silence that quickly became uncomfortable to anyone who had something to hide.

Samson withstood this technique for nearly a minute, but then made a pshaw sound. "Whatever. I guess there isn't much privacy anymore. I just wanted to have Mr. Butler either hire me or write me a recommendation letter. That's it. I figured I'd try to reach him at home so I went digging into property records. I went to one of his listed addresses last night, but Cornelius wasn't there. It was just some strange lady with a bunch of cats."

Cornelius's sister Olivia, I figured. Cornelius must have purchased her house for her if he was listed as the owner.

Burton lifted his eyebrows. "You used to work for him, then? You were an employee at his construction firm?"

Samson made a face like he had a bad taste in his mouth. "Yeah. Yeah, I worked for him. And it just about ruined my life. I figured the least the guy could do would be to write me a recommendation letter to show to another construction company. Or hire me back again."

Burton said, "Why did it ruin your life?"

Samson rubbed his face and suddenly looked very tired. I didn't know if that was because he was tired of telling the story or because he was tired of having lived it. He looked down at the driveway as if a way to phrase his story was down there and then looked back up at us again. "Cornelius was somebody who liked to work on a schedule and with real tough deadlines. He didn't ever want us to slow down or for the company to be fined for not finishing up a project when he'd said it would be done."

Burton said, "So he cut some corners."

Samson shook his head. "Nope. That wasn't Mr. Butler's style. His style was to work us all like crazy. And he'd hang out at whatever site we were working on and would fuss at us all if he thought we were taking too many breaks or weren't moving fast enough. He treated us kind of like machines."

"But you weren't machines." Burton tapped his pen against his notepad.

"Exactly. And things happen when workers don't get enough breaks or enough rest. They start making mistakes."

"Did you make a mistake?" asked Burton.

"Sure did. And it was a costly one . . . for me, anyway. I was rushing around like usual, Mr. Butler yelling and me and a couple of guys, and I lost my footing. Fell off a building from the second story."

Burton and I winced.

"Did Cornelius do all right by you?" asked Burton.

"Not really. I mean, I got disability pay and stuff. He called an ambulance and the hospital saved my life and helped put me back together again. But the accident kept me from being able to work for years. I had to move in with my sister and her family and totally lost my self-respect. I just recently got a small place of my own—that's how long it took to move out again. And all the time, my back was killing me. I had to go through physical therapy every week, chiropractic visits, and exercises at home. Since I couldn't work, I lost my health insurance."

Burton frowned. "So you've been trying to reach Cornelius."

"Just to see if he could rehire me or write me a letter, like I said. Construction is all I know how to do . . . I've been doing it my whole life."

I said slowly, "But surely—well, are you able to do it anymore? How is your back now?"

Samson shook his head. "It won't never be the same again but it's about as good as it's going to get. And I left on good terms with Mr. Butler. He was real worried about me for a time and visited me and my family when I was in the hospital."

I reflected that Cornelius had likely been trying to figure out if Samson had any intention of suing him or his company for pushing his workers too hard.

Burton sighed. "I hate to be the one to tell you, but Cornelius is dead."

Samson just stared at him.

Burton continued, "He was late for a meeting this morning and was found dead. The circumstances of his death seem suspicious." He gave Samson a serious look. "I need to find out where you were this morning."

Samson's dark brows knit together. "Hey, I didn't do anything to the man. I wanted something from him—I wouldn't have killed him."

Burton was quiet for a moment then said, "Maybe you caught up with him here at the house and he said he wouldn't hire you or give you a reference. That would be really infuriating, wouldn't it? Being treated that way after you'd been such a dedicated employee. I know I sure wouldn't think it was fair."

"But I didn't! I'm here because I didn't get the chance to talk to him yesterday at the library. It looked like he was busy talking with other people and he didn't look in a great mood, so I knew it was going to be pointless asking him to do anything. I drove over to his other house last night to have a word with him. And before that I was at home, just hanging around until coming by here."

Burton tapped his pen on the notepad again. "It sure does seem early in the day for you to come over here."

"I was just trying to catch up with him before he headed over to the library this morning. I know he'd go over there early, and I wanted to speak with him in private." He looked down at the driveway again. "I didn't want to have to beg in public."

Burton sighed. "I can't see why you'd want to go back to work for him after seeing what kind of operation he ran. That's got to have been stressful. Why subject yourself to it again?"

Samson shrugged. "Didn't really have a choice. I need to put food on the table. Besides, sometimes it's better to go with the devil you know—than the devil you don't—and I wasn't going to have any surprises with Mr. Butler. Anyway, he wasn't all bad. He never asked for anything he wasn't willing to do, himself.

He'd jump right in there with us sometimes, putting up scaffolding, clearing out sites, that kind of thing."

"So he was driven to work and thought everybody else should be as driven as he was."

Samson said, "Yeah. Like I said, I don't have any ill-will toward the guy, but I did think he owed me something for all the trouble he put me through."

"Do you have any thoughts on who *might* have harbored ill-will against him? Because it sure looks like somebody did."

Samson reflected on this for a moment. He said slowly, "Well, him and his sister didn't get along all that well."

I cleared my throat again. "Didn't he have more than one sister?"

Samson nodded. "That's right. I'm thinking of his older sister, Justine. She'd come out on the sites sometimes because she liked getting all up in Mr. Butler's business. She'd tell him what he was doing wrong, boss him around, and give him advice on running a business, even though he never asked for it. They didn't even pull for the same sports teams. Those two really didn't get along."

"Did it seem like his sister had it in for him? I mean, did she also have specific complaints or real beefs with him, or did it seem like minor stuff to you?" asked Burton.

"It seemed to me like it was more petty stuff. Although I felt like Mr. Butler did like to play people off of each other sometimes." He quickly added, "That was just a feeling I got—I don't have any examples."

Burton closed his notebook with a snap. "Okay, thanks. If you could, just give me your phone number and address in case I need to reach out to you in the future for any reason."

Samson did and then left with relief, glancing at them in the rear-view mirror as he drove away.

Wilson joined Burton and me, looking a little less-anxious.

"Did you get the staffing covered?" I asked.

Wilson gave a quick bob of his head. "Luna's heading there now and I've called in a couple of others." He rubbed the side of his face, looking at Cornelius's new home. "This is all such a shame. He was looking forward to spending time in this house."

Burton said, "So you two knew each other pretty well?"

Wilson shook his head. "Not *very* well—mostly in a business sense, although we were friendly, of course. Cornelius was the one heading up the library renovation work. He'd donated the materials and labor. I don't know what's going to happen now." Wilson's face was somber.

Burton's eyebrows raised. "I didn't realize the renovation had been donated. That must have cost him a mint—it seems like a lot of work they're doing over there."

Wilson gave a brief overview of all the construction crew was doing.

Burton said, "So your opinion of him was a good one, then? You and Ann, too? Both of you thought he was a good guy?"

Wilson said with a touch of asperity, "Well, I definitely didn't think he'd be murdered, if that's what you're asking."

"No, of course you didn't. But do you think he could have had any enemies? I just listened to a former employee of Cornelius tell me how tough he was to work for."

Wilson said slowly, "Oh. Yes, I imagine he could be a hard taskmaster. He certainly seems to expect a lot of his crew. I've heard him upbraiding them before when I've been walking by."

I nodded. "I thought he must be something of a perfectionist. He'd have crew members redo things right then if he thought they weren't done to his standards. But I really liked him—of course, I wasn't working for him. I thought Cornelius was pleasant to talk to and obviously very supportive of the library."

"And of all of us *in* the library," said Wilson, nodding his head. "We have a patron who's been giving us fits lately."

He looked over at me and I snorted. "This guy complains about *everything* but still comes to the library every day. It's either too hot or too cold in the building, too noisy, etc. Of course, we've done what we can to try and placate the patron and make adjustments to keep him comfortable. But one day Cornelius was near me when the patron came up to Wilson and me to complain about something and Cornelius just let him have it."

Wilson had a faint smile at the memory. "He told him that we were public servants and he should be grateful for us instead of giving us a hard time. Made me like Cornelius even more." Then his expression grew worried again. "And now I'm not sure what the status of the renovations will be. Will his generous donation be continued by the company?"

Burton said, "Do you have a contract?"

Wilson brightened. "Yes, of course. We have a contract for the work, so the company should continue the work, as per the document." He looked vastly relieved.

Burton said, "If you guys want to head out, you're welcome to do that now. Sorry I can't let you have the books just yet, but I can let you know when you're able to come back and collect them."

He was called back into the house by the state police and Wilson and I got into the car. On the way back, Wilson said absently, "The library will have to do something for the family. They're going to be devastated, I'm sure. And it's going to be important for us to maintain a good relationship with them through this. Should we order some food, do you think?"

I said, "That's the best idea. I can pick some up and bring it to the different family members. Since none of them even know about Cornelius yet, I suppose tonight or tomorrow morning would be the best."

Wilson nodded. "Let's see. He has the nephew, of course, who works with him. And then he has two sisters."

"Olivia and Justine," I said.

Wilson raised his eyebrows and briefly turned to give me a smile. "You have a good memory."

"Well, I was trying to make sure I remembered. Cornelius would chat with me sometimes in the library and I thought I should make some effort to remember the family members he'd mention. It seemed he and his family were very close."

"I thought so, too," said Wilson with a sigh. "Like I said, it will be quite a blow for them. And on a purely selfish level, it makes me anxious about the completion of the library renovation. I'm not as concerned it won't be finished since we *do* have that contract, but I'm worried that it won't be done as *well* if Cornelius isn't there to oversee everything."

I chuckled. "You've obviously heard Cornelius fussing at his nephew."

"That's exactly what I mean. It always sounded as if Cornelius was horrified by whatever mistakes Nate made. It makes me a little nervous about the future project."

I said, "The problem is that you and I don't know anything about construction. Nate might have been doing a perfectly good job and Cornelius was being a total perfectionist. Maybe Cornelius was just one of those people who wasn't really good at delegating and thought he could do a better job, himself."

Wilson said grimly, "Or maybe Nate didn't have a clue what he was doing. That's what makes me concerned."

He did seem to be getting wound up and I wanted him to focus on his driving so I changed the subject to library-oriented things and he seemed to perk up. Soon he was dropping me back off at my house.

"I'll be over at the library in just a couple of minutes," I said.

"Take your time. We do have extra help today, so take a minute, if you need it, and just clear your head."

I nodded, surprised. Wilson usually seemed to have a total work focus but lately I was seeing more signs that he was mellowing a little. Luna's mother Mona, who he was dating, must be having a good influence on him.

I ended up taking his advice and took a few minutes in my house to just relax. I made some Irish breakfast tea and snuggled with Fitz on the sofa while I drank it. He curled up as close to me as he could, tucking his furry head under my chin, which tickled, but not in a bad way. When I finished the tea, I put Fitz in his carrier, grabbed my lunchbox from the fridge, and headed to the library.

When I got there, I walked in and took Fitz out. I noticed that the construction crew was already there and working away . . . including Nate, Cornelius's nephew. My eyes met Wilson's from across the room and he winced and came over.

Chapter Five

IN A LOW VOICE, HE said, "Clearly, Burton hasn't had the opportunity to speak with the family yet. But it seems disingenuous of us to just carry on like nothing happened."

"I'll call Burton," I said.

Wilson gave a nod of his head and briskly walked to his office, carefully avoiding looking in Nate's direction as he passed by.

After Burton answered and I explained the situation he said, "Just hold on. I'll be right over there. The state police have got things covered here for now and it would be better for me to be the one to let the family know."

I carefully kept myself busy by checking in books that had been left in the book-drop the day before. About twenty minutes later, I breathed a sigh of relief as Burton came in.

"You can take him into the breakroom if you want," I said. "I'll unlock the room. It's too loud out here with the construction work to have that kind of conversation."

He nodded and I quickly unlocked the door to the lounge while Burton asked Nate if he could have a word with him.

Luna came over to the desk and gave me a look. "I can't believe Nate is here."

I shook my head. "Burton hadn't had the chance to tell him yet and Nate just came to work as usual."

"What on earth *happened*? All Wilson said was that there'd been an incident with Cornelius and you and he were going to be late. When I asked him what kind of incident, he told me he'd died."

I said in a low voice, "Burton thinks it's a suspicious death. Wilson and I found him."

Luna shook her head. "And both of you are here? Shouldn't you have taken today off? That must have been a real shock for both of you."

"It was, but I think we both wanted to keep busy today and working is the best way to do that. But I hope Nate's going to leave, at least for the day. I'm sure hearing about this is going to be upsetting to him."

Burton came out of the breakroom looking grim, with Nate following somberly behind him. Burton gave him his business card, scribbling something on it before he did. Then he walked toward Luna and me as Nate dropped heavily into a chair, looking a little dazed.

Burton brightened a bit as he spotted Luna and she gave him a cheery smile in return. I'd noticed that Luna was definitely warming to Burton, but not quite enough for him to feel comfortable asking her out yet—something he clearly wanted to do. Instead, he spent as much time as possible near her at the library. Hence, his sudden upgrade into "avid reader" category.

"How did that go?" I asked quietly.

Burton shook his head. "I don't think he's wrapped his head around it all yet. Maybe keep an eye on him. I advised him to go on home. The last thing he needs to be doing in his state is using power tools."

I grimaced. "And it was a matter of opinion whether he was even using those well to begin with."

Luna said quietly, "Do you have any leads yet?"

Burton shook his head. "It's early for that, although I wish we did. I've got to join back up with the state police and see what their forensic team has dug up. I've sent my deputy out to inform Justine and Olivia about Cornelius's death."

Burton paused for a moment, looking at Luna. For a second, I wondered if he was going to ask her to meet up with him later for a coffee or something. Instead, he hurriedly said, "Well, I should be getting along then. I'll talk with you later."

Luna watched him go, thoughtfully. "He must hate having to give family bad news like that."

"It's probably one of the worst parts of his job," I agreed.

"And this would be so hard to take in, wouldn't it? I mean, I can't even imagine someone murdering Cornelius. He was like everybody's favorite dad. He told me he liked the purple streaks in my hair when I changed from red to purple. He actually noticed! I mean, it's not even that much difference from red to purple. And he told corny jokes sometimes. Who could get mad enough at him to do something like that?"

I thought about his former employee. But he hadn't really seemed that mad, just desperate. I shook my head. "I have a tough time thinking of him having enemies, too."

Luna said, "He's not married, so it's not his spouse. He seemed like he was super-close and involved with his family, so it doesn't seem like they should be involved in something like that. Maybe it was a burglar or something? I know he must have had a lot of money."

I thought back to when Wilson and I were walking through Cornelius's brand-new house, looking for him. There had been all sorts of expensive things in every room. I said, "If it was a thief, it was a thief who didn't know what he was doing because he left a lot of really nice things that he should have taken with him."

"Yeah, that doesn't sound much like a thief. Well, I'm sure Burton will get to the bottom of it." Luna glanced up at the clock. "And I better get ready for storytime. At least the construction noise has died down a little bit. Last week, I thought I was going to have to use a megaphone to read the story just so the kids could hear me."

She rushed off, a blur of color as she went.

I finished up checking in books and was about to start scheduling social media posts for the library when Nate walked up to me. He gave me a small smile, his eyes looking red. "Hey there . . . it's Ann, right?"

"That's right," I said quietly. "I'm so sorry about your uncle. We all thought a lot of him here."

Nate nodded and used a finger to brush away a stray tear. "Thanks. I was wondering if I could talk to you for just a minute—if you're not too busy, that is. Am I interrupting anything?"

"Not at all," I said. He hesitated as if not knowing how to start and I said, "You must have had a terrible shock, hearing the news. Wouldn't you rather go home for the day? The work for the library can wait. It'll definitely still be here when you get back."

"Thanks. But I think you must have gone through a shock today, yourself, and you're still here." Nate had a stubborn set to his chin.

"That's true. I guess I was thinking that coming to work would be a good distraction for me and a nice way to stay busy," I said with a smile.

"That's the way I feel, too. I'm going to try and stick it out here today, although I might leave a little earlier than usual." He looked vacantly ahead of him. "I just can't believe he's gone. I was about to call him to see what the hold-up was because he was always here early. I don't think he'd ever been late for anything a day in his life."

I said, "That's what Wilson, my director, said, too. That's why we walked into his house to check on him. Wilson said it was very out of character for Cornelius to be late for any sort of meeting."

Nate nodded and started choking up. I said gently, "You must have been very close."

"I know he was my uncle, but he was more of a father figure to me," said Nate softly. "I just can't believe he's gone. And that somebody killed him . . . that's just unbelievable."

I said, "That's the part that got to me, too. Again, I'm just so sorry."

Nate paused to collect himself. "Now that it's sort of settling in, I'm trying to think who might have done something like this, you know? Who could have been so mad at him that they'd think they had to get rid of him?"

"Does anyone come to mind?" I asked. "Because, from what I've seen, Cornelius was a very popular figure around town. I've seen lots of our patrons go over to say hi to him and chat for a while when they've seen him in the library. He acted friendly to everyone."

Nate nodded and then his face darkened for a moment. "I guess it must have been Samson. I can't believe it, but I can't think of anyone else."

I decided not to mention Samson's visit at the library yesterday or the fact that he was at Cornelius's house this morning. I didn't know Nate very well and wasn't sure if he could end up being the vigilante type. I said instead, "Samson?"

"Yeah. He's a guy who used to work for my uncle for some years. He had an accident on-site one day and I guess he never really completely recovered." Nate shrugged. "Construction work can be dangerous. I think everybody who does it realizes that. It's not like some office job. Or working at the library."

I smiled at him. Working at the library could be more exciting than Nate imagined.

He continued, "Anyway, Samson got hurt and was on disability for a while, from what my uncle told me. Lately, he's been sort of making a nuisance of himself."

"How has he done that?"

Nate rubbed at his temple as if a headache was coming on. "Samson has just been lurking around. And Cornelius said he was leaving messages on his cell phone and texting him all the time, asking for him to meet with him." He brightened as a thought occurred to him. "The cops probably have Cornelius's phone, don't they? They should be able to see all those."

"I'm sure they do," I said. As long as the murderer didn't take it with him.

"Well, I'll leave that up to them, then," said Nate, sounding relieved. "That way I don't have to get involved. I wouldn't want to accuse Samson of something like that. When Cornelius was talking about him, I felt sort of sorry for him, actually."

Nate clearly *wasn't* the vigilante type. It sounded like he was more the polar opposite—someone who didn't want anything to do with it.

I asked him, "You haven't been in town long, have you? I'm sorry you've had such a rough start here."

Nate nodded. "Yeah, Pearl and I moved here just a few months ago. I worked in real estate in Georgia, but the jobs kind of dried up where I was because there wasn't a lot of demand. I tried to ride it out for a while by getting odd jobs to supplement my income, but that got old really fast. That's why I was so grateful to Cornelius for getting me started here."

I said, "He took you on as a sort of apprentice?"

"That's right. I didn't have a background in construction at all, but my uncle showed me the ropes." He gave a rueful smile. "Sometimes I think I wasn't catching on as fast as he liked, but I was trying. It's hard learning something completely different from what you're used to doing."

"I bet," I said. No wonder Nate had been struggling. That would be a lot of pressure at once—moving from another state, finding a place to live, getting settled in, and then learning a totally different trade—while being carefully monitored by the person who'd made it all happen.

"Now I'm not sure what's going to happen," said Nate. He shook his head. "With Cornelius gone, I don't have anybody to really coach me through this. He'd encouraged me to make the move, let my girlfriend, Pearl, and me stay with him until we found our own place, and then was showing me how to do everything. And who even owns the company? What happens with the projects we're working on?"

Wilson and I certainly expected the library project to continue, considering the contract. But I didn't say anything—I had the feeling Nate was stressed enough as the implications of Cornelius's death really started to hit him. Instead, I said, "I'm sure Cornelius's attorney will be able to let the family know exactly how everything will work."

Nate nodded. "I guess somebody like Cornelius would have had a will, all right. And a plan for the company. He's so organized all the time." He smiled a little bit and quickly brushed away another stray tear. "I remember I told him right after I moved here that I was having trouble sleeping at night. I'd wake up and I felt like my mind was just spinning with all the things I needed to do. He showed me his planner. Did you ever see it?"

I shook my head. I was curious—I was something of a planner geek myself, although I'd never really found one that was perfect for me. I'd been looking for something to help me organize things I'd read, things I'd wanted to read, possible workshops and classes the library could offer, etc.

Nate said, "I thought he'd come out with some leather-bound executive planner with all the bells and whistles, you know? It would have been the kind of thing I'd be almost intimidated to use; I wouldn't want to mess up the pages with my chicken-scratch handwriting. But instead, he showed me his composition notebook."

I lifted my eyebrows. "Really? You mean the same kind we'd use at school?"

"Exactly. He'd just sketch in the days of the week, putting important things like meetings, appointments, stuff like that at the very top under the day and date. Then he'd make a list of everything he needed to do in each column for each day. He left blank pages in between the weeks so he could make lists of things—packing lists for trips, notes he took from a doctor visit, stuff like that. He said he even kept the composition notebook next to his bed at night so that anything he was worried about went right into it. Said it solved his sleeping problems."

"Did you try it?" I asked.

"Yep. And it made a huge difference. Although I have a feeling my sleep problems are going to start up again tonight. Writing in a notebook isn't exactly going to help me out with processing this."

"Maybe if you did a little journaling in it? That might help."

Nate brightened for a moment. "That's true. I might have to give that a go." He glanced back over at the construction crew. "Well, I guess I better get back to it."

I said quickly, "Do you mind giving me your new address? The library wanted to bring food over to the family. We all thought a lot of your uncle."

"Sure, that'd be great," he said. I gave him a pen and some paper and he scribbled out his address and phone number. "I really appreciate it and I know Pearl will, too."

"How is Pearl getting settled in? Does she like Whitby so far?"

Nate winced a little, then covered it with a quick smile. "Oh, she's okay—it's probably taking her longer to get used to living here than she'd originally thought, but it's fine."

"Where in Georgia were you living before this?" I suspected I might know the answer.

"Atlanta," said Nate, confirming my suspicions. She'd been used to all the amenities of a big city. The slow pace and different offerings Whitby had probably paled in comparison, at least at first.

"Well, that's a big change," I said. "And then she's probably also had to get used to spending time with your family, I'm guessing. Did she know them prior to moving here?"

Nate shook his head. "No, we're just dating. I think if we'd been married it would have been different. She hadn't met them and so it was probably a lot for her to get used to at once. But she's fitting in all right." But his tone sounded doubtful to me as if he was trying to convince himself that was true. I wondered what kind of friction Pearl might have created, especially with Nate's mother, Justine. From what Samson had said, Justine sounded prickly.

Chapter Six

HE LEFT TO JOIN THE rest of the crew and I went back to work, too. There was an upcoming technology drop-in that I wanted to advertise on our social media. They'd become really successful events for us with patrons bringing in whatever device they were having issues with while library staff (and our teenage volunteer Timothy who was excellent with computers) took a crack at fixing them. But I'd noticed we tended to get the same people in every time. In the hopes of broadening our attendance, I wanted to promote the event on social media. And, of course, any successful promo from the library meant Fitz. He was key to getting our posts liked and shared and in getting the word out.

Fortunately, Fitz was in a very alert mood. I clicked my tongue at him and he immediately padded over and bumped his furry head against my hand. I rubbed him for a few minutes and then carried him gently to the technology room and next to a computer. Often, I'd bring a cat toy to capture his attention, but today he posed perfectly, completely engaged in the process and almost seeming to understand what I was doing.

I'd just finished up and had brought Fitz back over with me to the research desk when Grayson came in carrying his camera.

"Hey there," he said with a smile. "I thought I'd take a few pictures of the construction progress for a piece I'm doing for the paper. I might get a quote from Wilson, too, if he's in."

"He's here," I said. "Although go easy on him because he and I had something of a rough morning."

He came closer, leaning on the research desk. "What happened? Trouble at the library?"

I filled him in, and his face grew sober as I did. "That's awful. Are you okay?" He reached out and gave my hand a squeeze.

I nodded, squeezing back. "It was just a shock, of course. But we had the feeling something was wrong when Cornelius didn't answer the door. Wilson said he was always really punctual and I'd noticed that he was always here on time at the library every morning, too. But still—it was pretty bad. Wilson and I were shaken up."

Grayson said, "I'll have to talk with Burton about it and see what I can write up for the paper. Did it seem like a burglary gone wrong? A break-in that Cornelius interrupted? It sounds like it was a nice house and I can imagine that being a real target."

"I don't really know. Cornelius seemed to get along well with everybody. Of course, being as successful as he was, he could have had some enemies, I guess. Or maybe some people had grudges against him." I told Grayson about Samson.

"I can totally understand where Samson was coming from, though. He thought Cornelius could at least offer him a job or give him a good reference, considering he'd sustained an injury on the job. And if Samson murdered him, why would he return to the scene of the crime while the cops were there?" said Grayson.

I shrugged. "Maybe he knew he'd be a suspect anyway because he's apparently been calling and texting Cornelius a lot, asking to meet up with him. Cornelius has apparently been ghosting him . . . totally ignoring his messages. Samson even showed up at the library yesterday to see if he could catch Cornelius here, but got spooked because there were so many people around and he didn't want to make his request in front of them. If he did murder Cornelius, maybe he thought returning to his house would make it look like he had nothing to do with his death."

Grayson said, "True. But killing Cornelius really doesn't make a lot of sense. He was trying to get Cornelius to help him out. Now there's no way for him to do that."

"Unless he got frustrated with him and lashed out impulsively," I said. I shook my head. "But you're right. This still doesn't make sense, no matter how I look at it."

Grayson glanced across the library. "I see Cornelius's nephew is still working here today. Does he know what happened?"

"Burton came by just before you came in and told him. Nate said he wanted to stay busy today, which is why I'm still at work, too."

Grayson said, "You don't think Nate had any bad feelings toward Cornelius, do you? It sounded yesterday like Cornelius could have been a little rough on him—like he expected a lot from him. And maybe like Nate wasn't really catching on very quickly."

"I talked to Nate for a few minutes and he seemed like he was genuinely upset about his uncle's death. And maybe like he was at a loss, too. Now everything has changed and he doesn't know who's going to take him on as an apprentice now. He still needs somebody to learn the ropes from."

Grayson looked back over toward Nate as he gave an exclamation of frustration at something he'd just done. "It sure looks that way. Poor guy. He's got a lot on his plate right now." He shook his head. "It's too bad I never got that interview with Cornelius for the feature I was going to run in the paper. It would have served as a nice tribute for his family."

I nodded sadly. We were quiet for a few moments. I was glancing around the library, looking at the different patrons, and said, "The features you've done for the paper have been great."

"Why do I sense there's a 'but' coming?" asked Grayson with a grin.

"No buts. I was just thinking that maybe you'd want to widen the scope of what you're doing. After all, you're going to be running out of influential people in town soon . . . there are only so many of them. Maybe you could change it into profiles of interesting people or people who folks in town don't know that much about."

Grayson looked attentive. This was one of the things I loved about him—he was always curious, never dismissive. "That sounds intriguing. Who do you think might fit the bill?"

"So many people. I run across all walks of life here at the library, of course . . . some patrons are here for computer resources. Some are here for the events we run and to connect with other book or film-lovers. Some want audiobooks to listen to when they're exercising or doing housework. I see Mr. Trenton in here from time to time—he's the garbage collector for everyone who lives outside the city limits and has been collecting for decades. He's a really interesting guy to talk to but most people probably don't get the chance. Then there are people who've been living here for a little while and no one knows much about them . . . even me. Like our patron Linus Truman over there." I nodded toward the periodical section by the fireplace. Linus was sitting there in his suit, poring over a newspaper.

Grayson raised an eyebrow. "I've heard you mention Linus before."

"He's one of my favorite patrons now. But it took forever for me to know anything about him because he'd just smile politely at the staff and keep to himself. We don't really know much about him besides the fact that he now owns a dog, Ivy, and he lost his wife, who he was devoted to."

Grayson looked thoughtfully at him. "I wonder how he'd feel about a feature in the newspaper."

I said with a shrug, "He could be horrified since he's really private. Or he could feel pleased to be asked. I could carefully find out. He'd have to be approached the right way. I haven't even been able to get Linus to come to film club."

"That would be great if you could reach out to him about it. In the meantime, I'll get in touch with Mr. Trenton to see if he might be interested in a feature. Do you have any contact information for him?"

I pulled his business phone number up online and texted it to him right as Fitz jumped up on top of the desk to greet Grayson, who was a particular favorite of his. Grayson said gently, "Hi there, little man. Good to see you again." He looked up at me as he scratched Fitz under his chin. "Thanks for the number and for the ideas. I'll get started on that right away." He glanced over at Wilson's office. "It sounds like now might not be the best time for me to get that quote from Wilson. I'll give him a call later after he's had a chance to process this morning a little. But since I'm here and Fitz is in such a happy and alert mood, how about if I take some outdoor shots of him in front of the library? Wouldn't that fit in well with what the library is doing on social?"

"Actually, that would be amazing. I'd just taken a few photos of Fitz myself before you came in and he was in the mood to be a terrific model. And you've got your great camera with you."

"Do we need to wait for your lunch hour to do this? I could come back."

I said, "Ordinarily I'd have to make sure the desk was covered before I leave but no, I don't want to do library business during my lunch hour. It's fine if I walk out of the building for a few minutes because Wilson called reinforcements when we were held up at Cornelius's house this morning."

"Okay, great. If you can be the cat wrangler, I'll figure out a few good vantage points for the pictures, with the lighting and everything. It would be better if I had my portable reflectors with me, but I don't have them in my car."

I smiled at that. Grayson, in terms of his job, anyway, could be a bit of a perfectionist. "Hey, we're just doing a spur of the moment session with a cat. I'm sure the pictures will be a lot better than anything I could come up with, believe me."

I sent Wilson a text to let him know where I was if he needed me and found one of the other staff members to hang out at the desk. Then I gathered up Fitz and we headed outside.

Fitz was just as engaged outside as he'd been earlier in the technology room, even though there were a million distractions outside. He smiled a bit wistfully at a bird that was flapping by, but then looked back at us as if realizing there was a task at hand.

"He won't run away, will he?" asked Grayson with concern. "The last thing I want is to be responsible for the Whitby Library losing their library cat. I think Wilson would come after me."

I chuckled. "No worries. The doors open and close all day at the library and Fitz is never interested in leaving. And you're right about Wilson. He was very doubtful about having Fitz at the library at first, but then he quickly converted."

"What changed his mind?"

I said, "Well, Fitz's great personality, of course was a big part of it. But he also was fast to realize that Fitz could be a fantastic spokes-cat for the library and bring people in."

We put Fitz on the stairs of the library, and he sat regally, curling his tail around his feet. He still seemed to have a faint smile on his face as Grayson snapped pictures quickly from different angles. Then Fitz crouched down and looked intently at Grayson as he clicked the shutter.

I laughed. "Look how majestic Fitz looks! He looks just like the marble lions outside the New York Public Library."

"Even better than they do," said Grayson with a chuckle. He snapped off some more photos and then glanced at his watch. "Okay, now we're dangerously close to your lunch hour. You'd better go grab something to eat. I'll email you these pictures sometime this afternoon."

I said, "Thanks for this, Grayson. These are going to look amazing online. Fitz looked so animated out there and we've never done any exterior shots with him."

Grayson smiled and then said, "Well, I guess I better be on my way. Oh, hey, before I forget . . . did you want to go to that festival that's coming up? I figured with arts and crafts on display and music and food that we couldn't go wrong."

"I'd love to." This was a yearly festival for Whitby, which I loved attending, but I'd always gone alone before. That was fine, of course, and I still really enjoyed going, but it would be so much better to share it with someone. "Have you been to it before?"

He shook his head. "I'd moved here right after the festival last year. Okay, great! We'll plan on that. Hope the rest of the day is better than your morning was."

"It already is," I said with a smile, giving him a light kiss before Fitz and I went back into the building.

I was eating my leftovers in the breakroom with a now-sleepy Fitz dozing in a sunbeam when Wilson walked in.

"Are you doing all right?" he asked gruffly. "Sure you don't want to go home for the afternoon?"

"No, I'm doing fine. Are you?"

He sighed and smoothed down his already-smooth hair. "I suppose so. I've gotten a few things done anyway. How did the photo session with Fitz go?"

Fitz lazily opened an eye on hearing his name, then closed it again and rolled over to his other side.

I said, "It went great, although apparently we wore him out. He was really engaged out there, despite all the distractions. I think he's going to sleep the rest of the afternoon."

Wilson nodded absently. "By the way, after lunch, do you mind running out and picking up some sympathy cards for Cornelius's family and passing them around for everyone to sign? They can go along with the food that we deliver to them." He furrowed his brow. "Actually, that sounds like a lot. Do you need help with that?"

"No, it shouldn't be too much. I'll probably divide it up between today and tomorrow since there are several family members needing meals. And if I need a hand, I'm sure I could rope Luna into helping me."

"Good. Thanks for handling that." He shook his head. "It's all very unsettling, isn't it? I keep thinking that was a terrible way for Cornelius to go."

Falling down an elevator shaft was definitely not the best of ways. I'd been trying not to dwell on it too much. "I'm sure Burton will figure out who was behind this."

Wilson said, "It sort of reminds you of your own mortality." He gave me a small smile. "Well, maybe not so much for someone your age. But for someone my age, it certainly does."

This qualified as quite the heart-to-heart from Wilson. Emotionally, he often stayed as buttoned-up as the suits he was so fond of. I thought about my response. "I can understand how it would," I said slowly. "Maybe the best thing to do would be to take some time for something relaxing and distracting. Could you take Mona out for dinner? Go to a movie?"

He considered this. "There is an independent film and lecture that's going to be held over at the college tonight. I could ask Mona if she'd like a last-minute outing."

Knowing Luna, Mona had probably already heard about Wilson's rough morning. That meant she would likely be open to the idea of attending whatever Wilson was interested in doing. "You should call her," I said. "I'm sure she'd love to go out, last-minute or not."

After Wilson left to phone Mona and I finished up my break and ran the errand to pick up sympathy cards, the rest of the day was thankfully quiet. Nate, I noticed, slipped away at around four o'clock to head home, which I was glad to see. I was also on the schedule to leave at five, instead of staying to lock up at nine as was often the case.

Luna was leaving at the same time. We walked out to the parking lot together, me holding Fitz in his carrier, and I filled her in on the library errand I was running to bring food to Cornelius's family.

"I was thinking I'd take food by Nate's place first . . . he gave me his address earlier. Maybe a fried chicken dinner? I could make sure the restaurant gave us a lot of sides and biscuits in case he or Pearl doesn't eat a lot of meat."

Luna said, "Good thinking. Let me give you a hand with that. You've already had a rough enough day as it is."

I was happy to do some delegating since I was surprised to find myself already feeling pretty tired out. I took Fitz home and fed him while Luna picked up the food with the library credit card I gave her. Then she picked me up again and I navigated us to Nate's place—an apartment not far from downtown.

We walked up the stairs to their floor and knocked on the door. After a minute, the door opened and a woman with very blonde hair and lots of eye makeup stood there. She gave us a somewhat suspicious look until her gaze dropped and took in the bags of food we were carrying. "Can I help you?" she asked.

Chapter Seven

"PEARL?" I ASKED. "WE'RE from the library—Ann and Luna. We wanted to express our sympathy to you and Nate and bring you dinner tonight."

Pearl opened the door and gave a smile, although I noticed it didn't quite make it to her eyes. "That's nice of you. Come on inside. Nate's not here, I'm afraid."

We followed her into the apartment, which looked a little chaotic. It was clear that Pearl and Nate hadn't been able to unpack from their move yet. A couple of boxes were still taped and stacked along the walls, but most of them had been opened and the contents rifled through and spilled out the top as Pearl or Nate had searched for whatever item they needed.

It looked like Pearl was taking the edge off her day with a bottle of vodka that had been infused with raspberries. She glanced down at the bottle and said with a smirking smile, "Can I get you something to drink? Water? Coke? Vodka?"

I chuckled. "Tempting. But I'm fine right now."

"Me too," said Luna. "We don't want to take up too much of your time. We know it's been a hard day for you."

Pearl pulled a sad face, but there was a sly look in her eyes. "Isn't it so crazy? I'm sure it must have been an accident, no matter what the cops are saying. Cornelius had probably been tinkering with the elevator and simply forgot that it wasn't up on his floor. He was always messing with stuff. He'd probably been tweaking something with the elevator, that's all. The cops just don't have anything else to do around here and want to investigate it and treat it like a murder." She shrugged. "They might be bored and just trying to stir things up."

Luna and I glanced at each other. "Maybe so," said Luna. After all, if it made Pearl feel better to think it had all been an awful accident, who were we to make her think otherwise?

"Anyway, I'm sure it was an accident. But if anyone *did* murder him, it had to be Justine. She's Cornelius's older sister, you know. The two of them fought like cats and dogs."

I said mildly, "Brothers and sisters often do, don't they?"

"But these two were vicious," said Pearl, sounding a bit vicious, herself. "They fought about all kinds of stuff. Cornelius went to Clemson University and Justine went to the University of South Carolina. One of those 'house divided' things. They'd squabble over football like they were playing the games, themselves."

Luna said, "They might have felt really competitive with each other, I guess. Both of them ended up successful, too."

"Oh, you could tell they were competitive. Every single conversation was a game that they both were trying to win. If they were talking about college football, they were arguing about who was going to leave for the NFL. If they were talking about a mutual friend, they'd be throwing out all kinds of details to prove they were the better friend or knew the person better. It was constant."

"It sounds exhausting," I said. "But was it mean-spirited? You used the word 'vicious.'"

"Totally. I can completely see Justine getting mad at Cornelius in the heat of the moment and giving him a quick shove. I guess it's manslaughter then, but it's still not exactly a good thing." She quickly added, "But I still think it was an accident. Cornelius just couldn't leave anything alone. He was probably planning on fixing the elevator where he left off but had something else on his mind and forgot."

Luna and I glanced at each other. Could he have been thinking about the books and meeting up with Wilson and me and just absentmindedly wandered into an elevator that wasn't there? I shifted uncomfortably. It wasn't a pleasant thought. But, at the same time, it just didn't seem right to me. Cornelius wouldn't have been expending a whole lot of mental energy on our visit this morning. The books were already in boxes. He just had to show us where they were, say good morning to us, and we'd have been on our way.

I decided to change tack. "How has your move here been so far? It sounds like it must have been a real change from what you're used to. Atlanta, I think Nate said?"

Pearl made a face. "Yeah, it's been a change from Atlanta, all right." She looked at us for a second to make sure we didn't look defensive about Whitby and then added, "Some of the differences are great. There are absolutely no traffic jams here. Five o'clock traffic is just the same as traffic at ten o'clock in the morning. In Atlanta, it's just one big traffic jam where it's impossible to get anywhere any time of the day."

"But I'm sure other parts have been hard," I said, trying to sound sympathetic. The truth was that Pearl just didn't seem completely genuine to me, despite the fact she'd been pretty blunt during our conversation. There was a slyness in her eyes as if she were one step ahead of Luna and me. I had the feeling she probably was.

"Sure," she said with a shrug. "I had to leave all my friends behind in Atlanta and come here and start over. I have made a few, though. We actually were out late last night. We had supper and then went to some dive bar on the edge of town. So I've met some people and they seem like they might end up being good friends. But the rest of it has been hard. I didn't know Nate's family at all and they're all really close to each other. It's taken a while to feel like I fit in."

"But you do now," said Luna, always one to like a happy ending.

Pearl snorted. "Well, they tolerate me, anyway. I wouldn't say any of us are best friends. They're not the types to want to hang out all night at dive bars."

I noticed she hadn't said anything about Nate. "Are your new friends hanging out with Nate, too?"

Pearl shook her head and rolled her eyes. "Nate hasn't been fun at all since we moved here. He's had his nose to the grindstone the whole time and when he gets home, he's totally drained. That's why we haven't gotten anything unpacked yet."

It seemed to me that Pearl appeared very capable of getting the boxes unpacked and the things put away while Nate was at work. I thought I'd spent enough time with Pearl, especially after having a long day myself. I said, "Well, Luna and I should probably be heading out now. Again, we're so sorry about Cornelius."

Pearl gave us a perfunctory smile. "Thanks for the food . . . we really appreciate it."

Luna and I left and got back in her car. "Well, that seemed to go fine," said Luna with an air of relief.

"Were you thinking it might not?"

Luna said, "I don't know. I've seen Pearl before when she was bringing something to Nate at the library. I didn't get the friendliest vibe from her then. And obviously, she's forgotten that we've even met before. I mean, it was pretty brief and at the library and she clearly had something else to do, but I thought she *might* remember me."

Luna did, in truth, stand out a bit among the dark woods of the bookshelves and the muted colors of the furnishings.

"That's a strike against her," I said.

Luna, who was often more generous than I was, said, "It's not a big deal. Like I said, she was distracted."

To me, it indicated that Pearl hadn't found the encounter important in any way and promptly forgotten about it. But I didn't have very charitable views of Pearl based on our visit.

Luna gave me a sideways glance. "You didn't really care for Pearl, did you?"

"It wasn't obvious, was it?"

"Oh, no. But I can tell now. What's bothering you about her?"

I said, "I'm not sure. I think it was because I'd gotten the impression that she wasn't really telling us the truth. But then, I've had a really odd day and I'm tired and it's probably affecting my perceptions."

Luna said, "No, I understand where you're coming from. She was a little shifty. Plus, I thought it was crazy that she expected Nate to do all the unpacking and settling in. I mean—from what I understand, she has more free time than he does. Whatever! What's on the agenda for tomorrow's deliveries?"

"Tomorrow will be Olivia and Justine. I think I should call them to see what time works best for them for us to take the food by." While Luna was driving, I looked up their numbers on my phone and dialed them. Justine's was a very quick call, polite but succinct. She would like dinner and she'd be there after four o'clock the next day.

Olivia's call was a more meandering one and so Luna and I sat in my driveway while she spoke.

"Isn't it just terrible?" I could tell Olivia had been crying. "My big brother. Oh, I just can't believe this is happening! He's always been there for me and I couldn't be there for him when he needed me most!"

I felt bad for her—she obviously needed to talk it out and I wondered if she had anyone else to really talk to. She answered my unspoken question just a few moments later.

"I'm so sorry for talking your ear off. Goodness. It's just that Justine is always so clipped and inaccessible and doesn't like to listen to my rambles. I've already told my cats about it and they always look so understanding, but it's not quite the same, is it?"

I said, "No, it's not, although some cats can be excellent listeners. But Luna and I will be there tomorrow and would love to sit with you for a little while and you can talk just as long as you want to."

Olivia gave a big sigh of relief. "Will you? Oh, that's wonderful! Just wonderful. What time will you come?"

This was the crux of the entire phone call and I was relieved we'd finally made it to that point. "Well, we're bringing food on behalf of the library and we can deliver it and visit whenever it suits you best. What time do you prefer?"

"Could you come around lunchtime? That's just too sweet of the library to do that. Yes, lunchtime would be good. I'll have some tea for us, too—I have some wonderful boxes of teas." Her voice was suddenly anxious. "Do you like teas, though? I do have some coffee here somewhere. And wouldn't you like lunch, yourselves? I could round up some sandwich stuff." She sounded rather doubtful that she'd be able to, however.

"Luna and I will just eat before we come, but tea sounds great. We both drink it," I said, remembering all the tea I'd seen Luna drink in the breakroom.

Olivia happily rang off, now sounding much better with having something to look forward to.

Luna said with a wince, "Poor thing. She seems like she's really isolated there."

I said, "I know. I hope this is okay for your day off. I know neither you nor I are on the schedule for tomorrow."

"Oh, it's fine," said Luna waving her hand as if dismissing any thought of doing something fun instead. "She's sweet and she definitely needs an ear."

I climbed out of the car and Luna said, "See you tomorrow around lunch?" I nodded and she drove away.

There was a bright blue post-it note on my door with a heart on it and a scrawl I recognized as Grayson's. *Sorry I missed you* it said and had a sad face next to the heart. I took my phone out as I walked in the house and called him, but it went right to voicemail.

THE NEXT MORNING, I had a bunch of things on my to do list before lunchtime rolled around. I took my aging Subaru to the garage to get its oil changed. Then I had a dental appointment for a cleaning.

When I got back home, I pulled some weeds outside for a few minutes before heading indoors to get lunch and cuddle with Fitz for a while. He'd found the perfect sunbeam on the kitchen floor and was lying on his back, soaking it in. He made a trill when he saw me come over to him and I tickled him under his chin.

"I was going to brush you, too. Is that okay?" I asked him softly.

Fitz rolled over and watched me with interest as I rummaged around in the basket I kept cat things in until I found the brush. He actually liked being brushed, which definitely helped. He purred loudly as I gently worked through his fur.

I'd just finished when I got a text from Luna, letting me know she was in my driveway.

"Fried chicken dinner?" asked Luna as she backed out again.

"I guess. Olivia didn't seem to have a problem with it and neither did Justine when I ran it by her. It seemed rather unimaginative of us, but I don't know them well enough to have other ideas. Or ideas that don't involve us cooking."

"Perish the thought! I've been far too distracted lately to cook. I tried to make something for my mom last week and it was a total disaster. We ended up having to pick up takeout."

We got the chicken and headed over to the address Olivia had given me.

"Is this it?" asked Luna, sounding surprised when the GPS directed us to a particular house.

I peered at my phone. "That's the address Olivia gave me."

Luna frowned at the home, which was overgrown with ivy on the outside. Vines were scampering across the large bushes and stretched over the tall grass. "It doesn't really look as if anyone lives here."

I spotted a pair of eyes blinking at us from the base of a tree through the weedy grass. "We're in the right place. That's Tucker."

"Tucker?"

"The white cat over there. Olivia has shown me pictures of him. He's her favorite kitty."

Tucker gave us a disdainful look and bounded off in search of chipmunks in the undergrowth.

Luna put the car in park and said, "This is a far cry from Cornelius's place. At least, from what you've told me."

"Olivia is something of a character," I said with a shrug, picking up the bag of food. "I can sort of picture her living in a place like this."

Olivia greeted us at the front door with delight. When she led us inside, we could see that the inside of her house matched the outside. There were newspapers and magazines scattered around, a jumble of cardigans and rain boots in a corner, lots of used tea cups, and cats on nearly every surface.

Chapter Eight

OLIVIA SEEMED VERY pleased to see us and I wondered how often she had company. She bustled off to her kitchen, proud to be playing hostess and soon returned with more tea cups filled with herbal tea for us.

"Please excuse the mess," she said cheerfully. "The housekeeper hasn't shown up for a while."

I suspected there wasn't a housekeeper. Either that, or the housekeeper had declared surrender to the encroaching mess. Luna and I settled gingerly on the sofa after I inconspicuously moved some papers out of the way.

"Now then," said Olivia. "What do you think of all my little ones?"

We looked around us at all the different cats staring at us with interest from their various perches.

Luna said, "They're gorgeous. So sleek and beautiful."

And they were. Olivia might have ten cats, but they were clearly her babies and well taken care of. Much better, perhaps, than Olivia took care of herself. Her bun was askew, hair streaming out of the elastic band she was using. Her clothes, as usual, were a mismatched affair. But the cats were in wonderful shape and must be groomed daily, judging from the numerous brushes littering the room.

We sipped our herbal tea and chatted lightly for a bit about the cats, their names, and their very individual personalities and habits.

"That's Rita Hayworth," said Olivia in a placid voice.

"Is it?" I looked over at the tabby who was giving herself a thorough bath. Luna's smile broadened into a big grin as if she was now being completely entertained.

"Yes. Oh, you'll appreciate this, dears, as librarians. You do remember Hemingway?"

Luna and I did.

"Well, you may know that Hemingway had a place in Key West. He was married to . . . oh goodness, which one was it? Martha Gellhorn? No. Pauline Pfeiffer. Isn't that right?"

I passed the question along to Google on my phone and said, "It was Pauline in Key West, yes."

"And an old sea captain that Hemingway met in his favorite bar, Sloppy Joe's, told Hemingway about his polydactyl cats. With the extra toes, you know. Oh, it was all fascinating when I read an article about it! The captain gave Hemingway Snowball and Hemingway said, 'One cat leads to another.' Then there were lots of polydactyl cats!"

I wasn't quite connecting this with the tabby named Rita Hayward, so I was relieved when Luna said, "Was one of the cats named Rita Hayward, Olivia?"

"Yes! I mean, no. Actually, I'm not too sure. But he named the cats after famous people, so there might have been a Rita. Anyway, I decided it would be fun to carry on that tradition now so I've got a Cary Grant and a Katherine Hepburn and a Marilyn Monroe . . . it's so much fun. And they have the funniest adventures! I love watching them during the day and seeing all the different interactions they have with each other and with the great outdoors. I keep a little journal every day and one of my greatest pleasures is going back and re-reading all their exploits."

The various Golden Age of Hollywood cats milled around us, bumping up against us from time to time for a rub.

"So you enjoy old films, too?" I asked.

Luna chuckled. "Watch out, Olivia. You're about to get recruited to film club."

I gave Olivia an apologetic smile as her eyes twinkled. "Luna is absolutely right. But if you enjoy classic films, you'd be great for our group. We have a fun time—popcorn, old films, and good people having interesting discussions."

"I might have to give that a go," said Olivia, looking pleased at being invited. "Of course, I'm supposed to be looking for a job right now, but that can always be put off for another time."

Olivia seemed only too delighted to have an excuse.

Then I came around eventually, gently, to the purpose of our visit.

"We wanted to say, on behalf of the library, how very sorry we are that Cornelius has passed. We all enjoyed seeing him at the library every day."

Olivia's face registered doubt at this, but then she brightened and said, "How lovely that he was so affable there! Of course, he could be a very entertaining person to be around, couldn't he? And he was a very helpful man when he wanted to be. Not too much of a cat person, but he always knew their names and could recognize them on sight. He had an excellent memory, as I recall—a very excellent memory."

Olivia seemed to be searching hard to find good traits for her brother, which surprised me. He seemed to have done a lot for her, from what he'd told me in the past, and always seemed so congenial. As with my conversation with Samson, I wondered if Cornelius Butler had another side that outsiders didn't usually see.

Luna was prattling on about Cornelius and the wonderful gift he'd given the library and how nice the renovations were going to be after it was all over. "So I know," she said, wrapping up her soliloquy, "all about how helpful he is, just as you were saying."

Olivia gave a bob of her head and her wild hair bobbed, too. "Yes, indeed. And he gave me this house, you see? A sort of cat refuge. I wait tables from time to time but I don't really have a regular income, per se. Cornelius took care of my money worries by taking away the biggest problem, which was housing. Very, very generous of him, of course."

"Well, we're very sorry about his death. He'll be missed," said Luna.

Olivia sighed. "He certainly will be. I just couldn't believe it when Burton came over to tell me the news. Of course, I'd been home with my cats the whole night last night and this morning and so I didn't have any useful information for Burton. The only person I'd seen yesterday was a fellow who came by looking for Cornelius. But he was at the wrong house."

Samson, I figured. So at least he had a partial alibi for last night.

Olivia continued blithely on. "Burton wanted to know the last time I'd spoken with Cornelius and I think it must have been a week ago. Bette Davis had to go to the vet and Cornelius very generously offered to pay the vet bill." Olivia beamed at Bette, a shy white cat, as if Bette had been solely responsible for Cornelius's generosity, based on her cuteness.

"That was kind of him," I said in a gentle voice. And it was. Cornelius had clearly not been as crazy about cats as Olivia was, but wanted to make her happy by helping out with something that was important to her.

"That's right. And that's why I told Burton. Because, really, who would do that?"

Luna and I glanced at each other with confused expressions.

"Do what, Olivia?" asked Luna.

"Kill him, my dear," said Olivia. "It must have been an accident. That's what I told Burton. Cornelius had done too many favors for people and been too kind for someone to do something like that to him. It just didn't make sense."

I said, "He did seem to be in the habit of helping people. Nate was talking about how much he's helped him out."

Olivia smiled. "Yes, Cornelius stepped right up to the plate as soon as he'd heard that Nate had lost his job in Georgia. A terrible thing, losing a job. Poor Nate was quite panicked and not at all sure what to do. He was tossing around all sorts of ideas—going back to school, moving up to New York where a friend of his lived, taking on some temporary jobs until something permanent came up. When he broached these ideas to my brother, Cornelius immediately told him that he should come to North Carolina and he'd help him set up a place to stay and hire him on."

"It's lucky that Cornelius had an opening on his crew," noted Luna.

Olivia chuckled. "I'm not at all sure that he did, dear. But he made room for him, that's for sure. Although he told me in private that he wasn't at all positive Nate was cut out to be in construction. Apparently, Nate isn't very particular about getting exact measurements sometimes. And he isn't the perfectionist that Cornelius was. But the important thing was that Cornelius made the effort with him and brought him on, don't you think?" Her expression clouded up a little and she said slowly, "Of course, Nate's dating that Pearl. She's something else."

I thought Pearl was something else too, but I wanted to hear what sweet Olivia thought about her. Just then, though, a sleek black kitty jumped into her lap for a little love. Olivia cuddled it and said, "James Stewart! He's the most loving of the group. Always wants to see his mama and get a little snuggle."

We chatted about James, who was an extraordinarily snuggly cat, for a few minutes until Olivia looked at us a bit blankly. "I'm sorry. We were talking about something before James jumped on my lap. What was it? I've completely drawn a blank."

I cleared my throat. "I think you were talking about Pearl, Nate's girlfriend."

Again, Olivia's face clouded just a bit. "Oh, yes. Goodness. I'm sure she's a nice enough girl, but I can't help but wonder if she's the right person for Nate. Naturally, it's none of my business, but I can't help but care for Nate and want the very best for him."

Luna said, "Of course you do! We spoke with Pearl yesterday and she did seem very different from Nate."

Olivia nodded eagerly, glad not to be the only person who thought so. "Isn't she? Just a bit coarse, I think. Not at all like Nate. But I shouldn't really speak like this. I won't be like the rest of the family."

I asked, "The rest of the family?"

Olivia tutted. "They haven't been very welcoming to poor Pearl. Not at all. Cornelius wasn't fond of her, and Justine makes all sorts of faces when you bring up her name. It's a pity for Nate because he does seem so crazy about her." Her brow creased and she added, "And what's to become of Nate now? He's still learning how to do construction. I wonder what's going to happen to Cornelius's company? It's all so distressing."

I said, "Maybe there will be another experienced crew member who'll be able to take Nate under their wing." I wanted to hear more about Pearl, but I didn't want to seem to be pressing Olivia for information. Fortunately, Olivia was in a mulling-over mood and decided to offer more information right away.

"Goodness, I'm so glad you're both here. It's good to speak with someone outside of the family about all this. Justine was quite vicious about it all when I talked with her on the phone about poor Cornelius. She's quite convinced that Cornelius *was* murdered and that Pearl was the mastermind behind the entire thing."

Luna said, "Really? What makes her think that?"

"She's beside herself with grief, dear. But with Justine, it comes out in a very different way. Cornelius and Justine always squabbled with each other, even when they were children. They fought over all sorts of petty little things. But under it all, I knew that they were devoted to each other. They were so much alike, you know. Both so driven. Both had so much energy. And they were certainly competitive."

I said slowly, "So Justine is blaming Pearl for it all?"

"She is, dear. At least, she was doing so on the phone. She seemed in the frame of mind to blame just about everyone in town, though. Angry! I believe that's one of the stages of grief, though, isn't it? Anyway, she thought that Pearl cooked this whole thing up. That Pearl suggested to Nate that he call his uncle from Georgia and tell him he needed a job. That Pearl wanted Nate to take over Cornelius's very successful business and be the sole owner."

Luna frowned. "That seems weird to me, though. Pearl had to know that Nate wasn't equipped to take over and run the business. It sounds like he was still learning the ropes."

"Just the same, that's what Justine was saying. Like I said, she's just really struggling with her grief. Quite overwhelming, it is. Cornelius and I always got along, unlike Justine and him. He's always looked after me like the big brother he was. Of course, he encouraged me, too. He knew that waiting tables was starting to get painful for me and he tried to help set up job interviews for me." Olivia looked rueful. "I never seemed to get the jobs, though. I know I need to go out there again and look. It's just that I don't have any skills, I didn't finish college, and I don't use technology. It isn't a good mix."

It sounded challenging to me, for sure. But Olivia didn't seem too worried about it. I wondered how much support Cornelius had been giving her. The house was a huge gift, of course, no matter what condition it might now be in. But had he also been supplementing her income to help her get by?

Luna squished her face up sympathetically. "Sorry about the waitressing. I can imagine that standing on your feet all day would get rough."

Olivia nodded sadly. "It does. My feet and my back get the brunt of it, of course. That's why I don't have many shifts. I'm not sure I'm the best waitress in the world, unfortunately. I sometimes get mixed up with the orders. And I tend to talk to the customers quite a lot."

That, I could definitely imagine. I was definitely enjoying visiting with Olivia, but there were still a lot of errands and things I needed to accomplish during my day off. I managed not to glance at my watch.

"Ann and I stand up a lot at work too. I'm wearing really comfortable shoes, though. Maybe office work would suit you," suggested Luna.

"Could you work in Cornelius's construction office?" I asked. "I know you said technology wasn't your forte, but they probably have lots of filing and other things that need to be done."

Olivia made a face. "Justine would never allow that. She thinks I'm a total and complete disaster. I suppose she's not very far off the mark, at that. But I just don't have all the ambition that she does. I'd be happy just to stay at home with my cats and work the crossword and read books."

"Sounds like heaven to me," I said with a smile. And it did. I hesitated and then said, "Going back to Pearl. Did Justine say *why* she thought Pearl might have wanted to harm your brother? It seems like she would be doing Nate and herself a disservice, considering how he'd been helping them out."

Olivia's bright blue eyes were wide. "Oh, I suppose it has to do with the will, don't you think?"

"The will?"

"Yes. Cornelius had made a recent change once he became Nate's mentor. He was always very open with the family about the contents of his will, you see. Anyway, he said that he was going to put aside a significant amount for Nate to help him get on his feet again. Perhaps Pearl was simply trying to hurry things along?" She shook her head. "But, goodness, enough of that talk. What do you ladies think about your tea? I have to say I have a special liking of the vanilla chai. Such a lovely mix of flavors, isn't it?"

We talked a few more minutes while we finished our tea. Then I glanced over at Luna. "Well, I suppose we shouldn't keep you any longer, Olivia. Again, we're so sorry about Cornelius. I hope you'll come back to the library soon—we've got some wonderful new books that I think you'll especially like."

Olivia's face lit up. "Do you? I know we talked about the Regencies, but I've already finished that one you gave me."

"I thought I remembered that you also enjoyed portal-style fantasy novels?"

Olivia clapped her hands together. You'd think James, curled on her lap would have jumped, but the cat kept right on napping. Perhaps he was accustomed to such things. "Oh, I do love a good portal fantasy! When I was very young, I read *The Lion, the Witch, and the Wardrobe* and ever since I've loved that feeling of being transported from a very ordinary place to one that's quite extraordinary. That's really what reading is all about, isn't it? Armchair travel to all sorts of marvelous spots."

Luna and I took our leave, telling Olivia we'd show ourselves out so that she could keep James on her lap. She gave us a grateful smile in return.

Chapter Nine

AS SOON AS WE GOT INTO the car, Luna said, "Wow. I've never seen so many cats in one place before."

"I know. But they were definitely all taken care of and loved. They seemed sweet."

Luna said, "Well, she definitely took a lot better care of them than she did of the rest of the house. Bless her. What did you make of all that?"

"Another family member who mentioned Cornelius's death must have been an accident. But Burton seemed sure that it wasn't."

Luna said, "I wouldn't dream of second-guessing Burton. He always really seems to know what he's talking about."

"What did you make of Olivia's Evil Pearl scenario?"

Luna chuckled. "She said that wasn't *her* perspective. I think I could see Pearl doing that. Actually, I'm sure I could picture Pearl having that kind of motive, but I might just be letting my feelings about Pearl dictate my opinion."

"She's not the most likable person in the world," I agreed. "Although I'm not totally sure I see her as some evil mastermind planning to do away with her boyfriend's wealthy uncle in order to benefit from his will."

Luna dropped me back by the house and said she'd pick me up a few minutes before it was time to visit Justine. Then she scurried off to take her mom to a doctor's appointment.

I hopped in my own car and ran my errands. Then I returned home and did all the necessary chores while Fitz kept me company. Finally, I was able to reward myself for a little while by sitting in the back yard with Fitz in my lap while I read my book. I'd been in the mood for a comfort read. For me, that meant re-reading a favorite book of mine, often one from my childhood. So I was delving back into the world of *Little Women* and felt a part of the family—as if I were hanging out with Jo, Meg, Beth, and Amy while Marmee took loving care of us all.

I must have drifted to sleep at some point because when my phone went off, I woke with a start. I fumbled for my phone while Fitz watched me with his fuzzy brow furrowed in concern. "Hello?" I asked, somewhat breathlessly.

"Hi there!" said Luna brightly. "I'm out in your driveway." I was apparently still trying to shake off my nap because she added, "To go see Justine? Is everything okay?"

"Yes, sorry, I fell asleep. Ugh. I'll be right there," I said in a rush.

I gently picked up Fitz and carried him inside, locking the back door behind me. I quickly ran a brush through my hair and grabbed my purse before meeting Luna outside.

I gave her a sheepish grin as I climbed in the car. "Sorry about that."

Luna said, "Oh please, you made my day! You always have your act together and I'm the one frantically scrambling around. It's a relief to know that every once in a while, you can drop the ball, too."

"Believe me, it's more than every once in a while," I said ruefully. "Okay, so fried chicken again?"

It was just the easiest solution. We zipped by the restaurant, where the staff was getting to know us and our order by heart. Then we drove to Justine's house.

Justine's house was the complete opposite of Olivia's cottage and much more similar to Cornelius's lakeside mansion. It was also on the lake but was made of materials that helped it blend into the wooded lot it sat on. The yard was meticulously landscaped with a range of lovely hostas, hydrangeas, yew, and ferns. Justine herself was out there, wearing a large, floppy hat and tending to the hydrangeas. She straightened when she heard Luna's car. She was tall like her brother, wore glasses and a stern expression, and had the appearance of not suffering fools lightly.

"Now I feel like I've got to be sure to behave like a grown-up," muttered Luna.

I knew what she meant. We greeted Justine and brought the food up to her. She stood watching us with her excellent posture and I felt a little like a student in front of a teacher.

"We're so sorry about Cornelius," I said softly. "The food is on behalf of the library."

Justine softened for a second, giving a small sniff. "Thank you," she said in her subdued way. "Please, come inside."

It wasn't a question. Justine started striding toward her house and Luna and I scurried to keep up with her.

The inside of the house was just as immaculate as the outside. In fact, it had a rather sterile air, despite having a lovely view of the lake and mountains and exquisite furnishings and art.

Justine strode into the kitchen to put the food away and wash her hands. She called out to us, "Can I get you any drinks? I have sweet tea and I'm pouring myself some."

"That would be great," we said in chorus and then gave each other wry looks. Luna and I seemed very eager to please.

Justine returned with a small tray of sweet tea and some cookies, which looked homemade by someone. Justine, to me, didn't seem to be the cookie baking type, but I could easily believe she would excel at anything she set her mind to. She settled on a silk sofa and gave us a thoughtful look. "So . . . librarians."

Luna sputtered a little through her tea. I gave Justine a steady smile. "That's right."

Justine gave me a considering look. "What's that like?"

I had the feeling, judging from the look Justine was giving me, that she assumed the answer might be "very quiet." But it wasn't, actually. Besides, I was hoping to continue her family's close relationship with the library, so I took a moment to think about my answer.

I cleared my throat. "Well, I've really only worked at the Whitby Library, but from my experience the library operates as a hub for the community. We have readers there, of course, but we also have folks using our technology lab to search for jobs or just connect to the internet. Our research desk helps patrons learn more about diseases or conditions they or a family member might have been diagnosed with. And the children's department, which Luna heads, is devoted to literacy for our younger patrons."

Luna gave me an impressed look and even Justine didn't appear quite as disinterested in the library as she'd first appeared.

"And books—they're not falling out of fashion?" she asked in a drawling voice.

I could tell at this point that she was playing devil's advocate with me. I made sure there were no defensive tones in my voice when I responded. "Not as far as I've been able to tell. Of course, there are a variety of different ways to read books now. If someone's not interested in paper books, they can listen to audio versions or check out digital books from our catalog."

Now there was a gleam of interest in Justine's eyes. "That's good to know. I may have to spend some time poking around over there this week. I'd sort of imagined it a dusty place where you and Luna fussed at everyone to keep quiet."

Luna laughed. "Actually, the library is one of the most bustling places in town. I don't think we could keep it quiet if we tried. Although we do have a quiet section for those who are trying to study. It's popular, too."

"I suppose you're both experts in the Dewey Decimal System?" drawled Justine.

I smiled at her. "As a matter of fact, we use the Library of Congress classification. Most libraries do these days."

"Excellent," said Justine absently. I could tell her mind was already flitting over to other subjects. She said, "Olivia called to tell me you'd brought her food earlier, too. That was very kind of you—and now here you are delivering a meal to me, too."

"We're happy to do it. And, again, we're so sorry about Cornelius. We were all very fond of him at the library."

There was a slight smirk on Justine's face. "Well, I'd imagine so. He made that big donation of materials and labor for the renovation work in there."

Luna and I looked at each other and Justine waved a hand dismissively. "Oh, ignore me. I'm not meaning to be catty. Believe me, I know how charming Cornelius could be when he wanted to be. It's very difficult for me to grasp that he's gone. I keep having the feeling that he'll barge through the door with a big grin and tease me about something or other."

"It must have been a terrible shock," said Luna soberly.

Justine gave a sniff again and I could tell she was trying hard to maintain her composure and keep her emotions at bay. "It was. I couldn't imagine for the life of me what Burton was here for when he showed up at my door yesterday. I only wish I'd had more information for him in terms of who might have done such a heinous thing."

I said, "So you don't think it was an accident?"

Justine looked at me as if I'd suddenly grown two heads. "Well, of *course* it wasn't an accident. Cornelius was *never* sloppy."

I quickly added, "It's only that others have mentioned that Cornelius enjoyed tinkering with things. They thought maybe he'd simply been absentminded and forgotten that he'd changed the settings on the elevator."

Justine gave me an icy look. "Absolutely not. Whoever said that is completely delusional. My brother was *never* absentminded. It's true that he liked tinkering with things, but he would never have been so careless as to leave a piece of equipment in a dangerous spot. Never."

I swallowed. Justine was quite fierce. Luna came to my rescue.

"So you believe his death was intentional, then? That someone murdered him?"

Justine still had a disdainful look on her face, but the disapproval was receding somewhat. "It's more likely that someone killed him than he was careless. I've spoken with Burton and have full faith that he and the state police are going to track down the perpetrator and make sure he sees justice. The family *must* have justice for Cornelius."

I nodded, wordlessly. Justine seemed very touchy and I didn't want to exacerbate anything. I decided to err on the side of caution and let Justine or Luna speak.

Justine sighed. "I'm sorry if I seem tense. I've taken Cornelius's death quite hard and am still trying to let it sink in. I had a special bond with him since we were close in age. We did tend to fight like little kids sometimes, but we shared a bond that we didn't have with anyone else. We saw the world through the same lens, if that makes sense. Whereas Olivia . . . well, you've seen her. Bless her heart. She's always been such a mess. It's as if Cornelius and I took all the initiative and she was left with nothing."

Luna said brightly, "Well, she seems happy, though! That is, she obviously isn't happy about your brother's death, but she is happy with her life."

Justine snorted. "Surrounded by felines. Yes, that's Olivia. She would be content anywhere as long as she had a little patch of land and cats all around her. The poor thing, her life has been one tragic event after another."

I dared to speak up again. "I'm sorry, I didn't know that. What happened?"

"Oh, just bad luck," said Justine, waving her hands vaguely. "She dropped out of college, went through a series of jobs, a series of relationships. She's at the point where she needs cash and quickly, but that hasn't really been forthcoming because Olivia would rather stay inside and visit with her animals instead of work. She has this habit of putting off indefinitely whatever she doesn't want to do . . . like work. Cornelius, for one, was exhausted from bailing her out. He'd purchased her house, helped her out financially from time to time, but was not happy having her calling him all the time and telling him she needed money for a house repair or to get her car fixed. He was over it. He'd told me he planned on confronting Olivia about it and telling her he was going to cut her off."

"That's a lot of support," I murmured.

"Yes, especially for someone who's your sister and not your child. But Cornelius was like that—he enjoyed helping people as best he could. I, on the other hand, felt Olivia was an adult and should be able to get herself out of her own messes. She should at least be able to find herself a job. Or be able to hold one down. But Olivia's modus operandi has always been a cycle of finding a job, not showing up for the job, then losing the job." Justine gave an exasperated grunt.

Luna and I weren't sure what to say to that, so we just nodded sympathetically.

After a few moments, I said, "Do you have any thoughts about who might have done this, since you think it was foul play? Did Cornelius ever mention being worried about his safety?"

"Never," said Justine brusquely. "You probably know how Cornelius was, having spent so much time in the library with him. He was a larger-than-life figure. It's hard enough for me to imagine him dead, much less murdered. But I have wondered over the last day about one particular person. He's a former employee and a disgruntled one."

I decided not to say anything about having spoken with Samson, although I had the feeling that's who she was referring to.

Justine confirmed it a second later. "His name is Samson, I think. I've noticed him hanging around Cornelius's new house lately. He was there once when Cornelius and I were taking a look at the construction progress before it was done—I suppose he'd followed us there. Cornelius wasn't worried about his safety, as I mentioned, but he did complain that Samson was harassing him with phone calls, emails, texts, and whatnot. Anyway, I mentioned it to Burton and I'm certain they will be getting in contact with him. The evidence is all there on Cornelius's phone and computer."

Luna said, "That's just awful. You'd think Samson would leave him alone after Cornelius asked him to stop contacting him. That sounds like a lot of harassment."

Justine sighed. "Yes, but that was part of the problem. I *told* Cornelius to tell Samson off in no uncertain terms. But Cornelius said that he was just ignoring the communications and felt Samson should get the hint. Samson clearly *wasn't* getting the hint, as I told my brother repeatedly. But Cornelius could be a very stubborn man. It was a trait that likely helped him in the business world, but didn't do him any favors in this instance. I feel sure that Samson, desperate to hear from Cornelius, approached him at the house, forced his way in, and facilitated his fall."

I said slowly, "But wouldn't that require some set-up? Samson had to have been in Cornelius's house prior to his death to lock the elevator mechanism."

Justine waved her hands airily. "When a house is still experiencing construction, there are many workers coming and going. The house was open much of the time. It wouldn't have required a lot of forethought and Samson was in the business, after all. He would easily have been able to walk in and scout out the place."

She gave a pointed glance at her watch and Luna and I hastily stood. "We should get going," I said.

Justine gave us a perfunctory smile. "I do appreciate the food so much. Please let the rest of the library staff know. It was very thoughtful and kind of you."

We took our leave and climbed back into Luna's car. Luna said, "Whew. I'm glad to get out of there. How on earth could she be related to Olivia? They're 180 degrees different from each other."

"They really are. Personality-wise, especially. Olivia is so warm and Justine is so remote."

Luna said, "Totally. And Olivia's house was all cozy and cluttered and covered in cats. Justine's house felt almost institutional, didn't it?"

"It was pretty sterile," I admitted. "But the important thing is that we passed on the library's condolences and have seen everybody in the family. Wilson will be pleased."

Luna was still mulling over Justine, apparently. But for a free spirit like Luna, Justine must seem very exotic. "So, what do you think Justine's deal is?"

"Her deal?"

"Yeah. Did she just not like us or is she like that to everyone?"

I said, "That was the first time I'd officially met her. Or unofficially met her, actually. I've seen her at a distance at lunch with Cornelius before, coming out of a restaurant. But she's obviously not a patron at the library."

"No. Although I did see a lot of books and they looked like they were read. But I think Justine's the kind of person where, if she wants to read a book, she just goes ahead and buys it. She's not going to the trouble of requesting it at the library, waiting for it to be put on hold for her, and then checking it out."

I said, "It looked like she had a lot of nonfiction—biographies of successful businesspeople and that kind of thing. I'd liked to have been able to browse through her books a little."

"A window to her mind would be nice," agreed Luna. "She's a hard nut to crack. We keep hearing how she and Cornelius fought all the time, but it sounds like they were really close, too. I guess it's possible to do and be both."

Luna and I were both only children, so we didn't really know personally. But I knew I'd seen enough siblings during library storytimes to understand what sibling rivalry was all about. "Like you were saying, they were both really different from Olivia. It was probably good for Olivia that she *was* different. It would have been hard to compete with those two. They were both so driven and competitive. No wonder they were always fighting with each other or trying to show up each other."

"What is it that Justine does again?" asked Luna. "It seems like she should have a high-powered job, but it's hard to manage that in Whitby."

"Cornelius told me she was an attorney. But she left for years to live in New York before coming back here. She's retired now and decided to come back home. It was interesting to me that she was the one person who didn't think Cornelius's death was an accident. Everybody else was convinced he'd been tinkering with the elevator, left the safety mechanism off, and absent-mindedly stepped into the elevator," I said.

Luna said, "Yeah, she was *not* pleased when you even suggested it could be an accident. She's pretty defensive about him, which I get. But she was really hostile when you mentioned the possibility of Cornelius somehow being careless in any way."

"And she's right. He might have been one to tinker with stuff or never leave well enough alone, but he was also extremely Type-A about everything. I can't picture him wandering away after leaving the elevator in a dangerous position and becoming distracted by something else. It doesn't fit in with his personality. But the reality of that is that somebody came into the house, set the elevator to remain on the bottom floor, and waited for Cornelius to step inside."

Luna pulled into my driveway. "It sounds like it might have been easy to accomplish that, what with all the construction workers being there."

"Exactly. No one would even have really noticed an additional person being inside. Okay, well, thanks for all the driving around today. See you tomorrow at the library."

Luna waved as I walked to the front door. Fitz was sitting in a sunny windowsill, watching contentedly as I unlocked the door and stepped inside. I sat on the floor in the small foyer and said hi to Fitz after he padded over to me.

Chapter Ten

WHAT I MOST WANTED to do was to curl up and read my book with Fitz. But what I most *needed* to do was to mow my grass. I didn't want to incite the wrath of Zelda. I threw on my yard clothes and fired up the push mower. The grass was still a little soggy so it wasn't the cleanest looking cut, but at least it wasn't tall anymore. I finished up by pulling a few errant weeds in the front flowerbed.

My cell phone started ringing as soon as I headed inside. I groaned when I saw who it was. "Hi, Zelda," I said through clinched teeth. "I took care of it, by the way."

Zelda said haughtily, "Took care of what?"

"My grass. I know it was super-long. Isn't that what you're calling about?"

"I'm afraid it's yet another infraction." Zelda put a good deal of emphasis on *another*.

My head started to hurt and I absently raised a hand to rub my forehead. I groaned again when I realized I'd rubbed mud into my eye. I reached for a paper towel. "An infraction?"

"Perhaps infraction is the wrong word. It's really a complaint from a neighbor."

I felt guilty already. The last thing I wanted to do was to create a problem for anyone. "Oh no. What have I done?"

"The front porch light. I know you like to keep it on and I can completely understand that, as a single woman, myself."

I reached up to rub my forehead again, this time managing to stop myself before smearing more mud on my face. I got another paper towel for my dirty hand. "Should I not leave the porch light on at night?"

"It's really fine. The issue is, though, that the light is flickering. Miss Hobbes was saying it was creating quite a strobe effect through her bedroom window."

I bit my lip. Poor Miss Hobbes. She was a very quiet woman and a regular patron at the library. She was so meek that it must really have been bothering her for her to reach out to Zelda and say anything.

"Sorry about that. I'll get that fixed."

Zelda abruptly hung up and I sighed with relief and hopped into the shower.

Once I'd gotten ready, Grayson called and invited me out to a spur-of-the-moment dinner. At least this time there were no obstacles to get in our way.

"Are you up for going for a drive to a nicer place? Or is Quittin' Time all right?" he asked.

Whitby was a great town and I loved living here. The mountains, the lake, the people were all fantastic. But it didn't really have many options in terms of dining. Quittin' Time was usually our place of choice, simply because we didn't have to drive to another town to go there. The only other option for sit-down dining was a place that was so formal it was usually reserved for weddings. It wasn't much in the budget of a newspaper owner or a librarian.

"How about if we do something a little different?" I suggested slowly.

"I'm all ears. You know this town a lot better than I do."

I said in a wry tone, "Unfortunately, I'm not able to come up with a lot of alternatives. But how about if we pick up takeout from Quittin' Time and go out to the lake? There are benches we can sit on over there and I bet the sunset is about to be gorgeous over the mountains."

Grayson said happily, "Perfect. Let me do the legwork. What would you like to eat? Do you need to look at the menu?"

Sadly, since I'd been there a million times, I *didn't* need to consult the menu. I gave him my order of a veggie plate with a cornbread muffin.

Just a short while later, we were out by the lake. Grayson had brought some seat cushions from his patio and scattered them over the bench. He had two bags of food and a small cooler. "I thought a little wine might hit the spot," he said with a grin.

"Perfect," I said with a contented sigh as he brought out some acrylic plates and wine glasses he'd brought along.

The sun was setting over the lake and the mountains in the background. The sunset was all cotton candy colors of pinks and blues and we talked about music—favorite bands from when we were growing up and how our taste in music had changed over the years. When I was a teenager, I'd liked songs based more on their beat and the energy behind them. But now, I was more focused on lyrics and tended to listen to music from real songwriters.

Grayson said, "And books? Has your taste in reading changed, too?"

I laughed. "You'd think so, but it's the same as it ever was. I read pretty much everything. I have my favorites, of course, but I like reading a variety of different genres and switching from fiction to nonfiction. I go off of recommendations, too—if somebody tells me a book is good, I'm going to read it, no matter what genre it is."

Grayson stretched an arm behind me on the bench and I rested back against it. It felt good to be sitting here at the end of the day with someone I was feeling closer to every day.

He said, "I'm trying to get to that point. I want to broaden what I'm reading but then every time I head into the library, I end up with a police procedural mystery."

Grayson looked so rueful that I laughed again. "There's nothing wrong with police procedurals. I read a lot of them, too."

"Yeah, but the difference is that you're reading other things, too. Maybe you can point me in the right direction," he said, giving me a smile.

"Of course I will. But you have to promise that if the book isn't sucking you in, return it to the library and let me find something else for you to try. There are so many great books out there and not every book is for every person."

We finished up our meals in a contented silence, watching the palette of the sunset change as the sun continued going down. There was a woman walking a dog around the lake and the dog was practically skipping, it was so happy. I knew the feeling and, looking at Grayson's face, I had the feeling he did, too.

The next couple of days passed uneventfully. And, actually, pretty quietly. The construction at the library stopped. This worried Wilson until he called the construction office to check in. Justine had been there and assured him that the work would resume in the next few days. In the meantime, she was trying to make sense of the business end of things and see what they had on their plate for upcoming projects. Wilson's relief was palpable when he filled in Luna and me.

We had the technology drop-in at the library and once again, it was a roaring success. Patrons brought in phones, laptops, tablets, and lots of questions. Fortunately, I had plenty of staff there to help out, as well as a couple of volunteers. Everyone seemed to leave happy with their devices up and running again.

Justine called into the main number of the library one afternoon and I quickly said, "Hi, it's Ann. Would you like me to patch you through to my director, Wilson?" I figured she was probably calling regarding the stalled renovation work.

"What? Oh, no, no. I'm not quite ready to address the work on the library at this point in time. No, I've been moving on to other things in the interim and one of them is Cornelius's effects."

It seemed like a fairly cold way to talk about Cornelius's personal things in the brand-new house he'd constructed and was so excited about, but tragically only lived in for such a short period. "Of course."

Justine continued, "I believe Cornelius was in talks with the library about the boxes of books he had."

"That's right. We said we'd be happy to take whatever books he wanted to donate to us for the Friends of the Library sale. The money raised from that will benefit the library."

Justine didn't seem particularly interested in the details of where the funds would be going. "Fine, yes. I was hoping you could meet me at my brother's house tomorrow morning for the books. I'll be adding some additional titles to the ones that he already boxed up."

"Absolutely," I said quickly. "Just give me a time."

"Would eight o'clock work?"

That was the time that I was to be opening up the library tomorrow. But I had the feeling that Wilson would, under the current circumstances, encourage me to do whatever Justine wanted. "That's great."

"See you then," she said, abruptly hanging up.

I walked over to Wilson's office and waited for a few moments for him to get off the phone. I filled him in on the plan for the next morning and he nodded his head. "Yes, whatever Justine needs. I'm hoping she gives the renovation work the green light soon. I'll get someone else to open for us tomorrow morning."

And so, with everything in place, I went back out to the reference desk and finished up what I'd been working on—my regular piece for the newspaper on book recommendations and upcoming events at the library.

The next morning, I woke up especially early. Justine wasn't one to mess around and I didn't want to be in the position of rushing around to get ready. I got up and got ready, then went into the kitchen and proceeded to make myself a full breakfast and a coffee that was a little darker than I usually drank. Fitz was still sleepy. He nibbled at the food I gave him a bit half-heartedly, then curled up in a kitchen chair for a nap. It looked like he was chasing birds in his sleep as his furry feet twitched.

I looked at my watch and decided to leave early for Cornelius's house. It wouldn't take me that long to get there, but I decided I'd be more relaxed if I got there early and just read my book until Justine arrived. I had the feeling she was the kind of person who put a lot of stock in punctuality. I put *Little Women* in my purse and climbed into the car.

For the drive over, I listened to a playlist that Grayson had made for me of some of this favorite music. Since his tastes were so eclectic, it made for an interesting drive to Cornelius's house. The playlist was full of jazz, blues, country, and pop and I was able to sample a few of the songs on the way over.

I was glad I'd gotten there early when I saw Justine's car already in the driveway at Cornelius's house. I pulled in and parked and gave her a smile. She raised her eyebrows and smiled back.

I rolled the window down. "Good morning, Justine. Sorry I'm a little early. I brought my book so I can read for a few minutes if you have other things you need to do here, first."

Justine gave me that tight smile again. "No, that's fine. Since you're already here, it makes sense for us to go ahead and get started. I'll see to the other things later."

I'd been so focused on Justine that I hadn't noticed the older-model sedan parked at the very bottom of the driveway. "Looks like someone else is here getting an early start."

"Yes," said Justine brusquely. "It appears Pearl is here. I can't for the life of me imagine why. *I'm* the one going through Cornelius's things. I guess she must have used Nate's key. At any rate, I'm going to find out what she's doing here. She's not even family."

I wasn't quite sure what to say to that, so I just nodded and followed her in. She walked briskly in on the ground floor and had no hesitation about using the elevator. I quickly followed her. She was clearly too practical to worry about such things and the elevator would certainly make transporting books a lot easier.

Justine was tapping her foot as we went up for the short ride in the elevator. I could tell she was impatiently waiting for the opportunity to give Pearl a piece of her mind.

As the doors opened, Justine immediately called out, "Pearl! Pearl Ross. What in heaven's name are you doing here?"

There was no answer. The hairs on the back of my neck started to stand up at the similarity with Wilson's and my arrival at Cornelius's house the last time and finding him. But I reminded myself Pearl was not Cornelius. Besides, if *I'd* been Pearl, I'd have been trying to hide, given the tone of Justine's voice.

"Where is that woman?" muttered Justine.

I decided to just stay out of the way and let Justine do her canvassing.

"I do *not* have time for this today," said Justine grimly as she opened doors and peered inside, eyes narrowed.

I glanced across the room at the glass doors leading to the second story deck. "Maybe she's taking a walk on the trails by the lake."

Justine scowled at me and I said feebly, "At least, I think there are trails, aren't there? There seemed to be."

"Yes, but that would be a silly thing for Pearl to do. I can't imagine her driving all the way out here just to exercise outdoors. Plus, it's very early in the morning and Pearl is simply not a morning person. No, I think she's here snooping—trying to be here while no one else is around. She just happened to underestimate me because I actually *am* a morning person."

I walked out the doors and onto the deck, mostly to stay out of Justine's way and to give her the opportunity to calm down—or to find Pearl and give her a piece of her mind without my being there. It looked like it was going to be a beautiful day—the sun was starting to rise over the lake and I could see the light dappling over the nooks and crannies of the mountains behind the lake. There was a soft breeze.

Cornelius had put a good deal of time into designing the landscaping, or in hiring someone who knew what they were doing. The yard sloping down to the lake was expertly crafted and seemed like a natural part of the surroundings. I glanced down below the deck and froze.

Pearl Ross was sprawled on the rocky ground two stories below.

Chapter Eleven

"JUSTINE!" I CALLED, fumbling for my phone to call Burton. I doubted very much that Pearl would have jumped off the deck herself, so the house was a crime scene. Plus, there was a chance that Pearl was still alive.

Justine snapped from behind me, "Well?"

I turned around in irritation although Justine couldn't have known what had happened. "Pearl is lying on the ground below."

Justine became silent and followed me as we hurried down the exterior stairs from the deck to the ground. I gently felt for a pulse, but couldn't find one. Her skin was cool to the touch. She was lying face-down on the ground and I could see there was some sort of injury on the back of her head. "I think she's dead," I said soberly.

I called Burton. Justine walked away from Pearl's body toward our cars, whether in shock or from a desire to keep a crime scene untouched, I wasn't sure. A minute later, I joined her.

Justine said in a stilted tone, "It seems unlikely she jumped."

I nodded. "There was also an injury to the back of her head."

We were quiet for a few moments. It seemed hard to believe that this beautiful, peaceful setting would have another victim on its property.

"What do you think she was doing here?" I asked.

Justine held out her hands. "How would I know? I assume she was doing what everyone else was doing the past few days—taking things from the house before Cornelius's will is even read."

I raised my eyebrows. "The family was doing that?"

"Of course they were," said Justine briskly. Some of the color she'd lost was starting to return to her face. "Possession is nine-tenths of the law, after all."

We were quiet until Burton arrived. Justine's tight expression made it clear she wasn't in the mood for conversation and I was feeling slightly sick at the horrible sense of déjà vu I was experiencing. Burton drove quickly up minutes later, lights going but no siren. He got out of the police car and gave us a grim look.

"You both okay?" he asked gruffly.

We nodded mutely and I pointed out the direction he'd need to go in to find Pearl.

Justine walked silently away to sit in her car and stare blankly out the window. I leaned against my Subaru, waiting for Burton to return.

He came back around and stretched out crime scene tape. Then he made a phone call. Finally, he came back over to speak with us. He spotted Justine sitting in her car and motioned me over so that he could speak with both of us at the same time.

Burton spoke with me first. "Since you're here, Ann, I'm guessing this visit to the house had to do with the books again."

I cleared my throat. "That's right. Justine called me yesterday at the library and asked if I could meet her here to remove the books Cornelius had set aside and some additional ones she'd wanted to send along."

"Were you planning on meeting Pearl here?" asked Burton.

Justine jumped in, icily. "Definitely not. Pearl had no business being here. She's not family and no one asked her to go through Cornelius's things. I was surprised and displeased when I saw her car here. I called out for Pearl when we entered the house, but received no answer. Ann was out on the deck and spotted Pearl on the ground."

Burton nodded. "And what went through your mind?"

"Well, I know it certainly wasn't suicide. It's not enough of a drop for anyone to be able to count on dying from it. And Pearl thought way too much of herself to kill herself, that's for sure. I can only assume that someone met Pearl out here or followed her out here for the express purpose of killing her."

Burton nodded and jotted down a few notes in a small notebook he'd removed from his shirt pocket. "What was your opinion of Pearl?"

Justine sighed and rubbed her forehead distractedly. "To be perfectly honest, I was less than enchanted by the young woman. I thought my son could do far better than Pearl. But Nate has always been susceptible to calculating women."

"Calculating?"

"Of course. Pearl wasn't from money or even a good family. She was trying to use Nate to live a better life. I'm not saying

Pearl didn't hold Nate in some affection—I believe she did, certainly. But that doesn't alter the fact that she was using him."

Burton nodded. "So what do you think Pearl was doing here at the house?"

"Well, she was either here to take things that she could sell later, or she was here to meet with someone."

Burton raised his eyebrows. "Who might have she been meeting with?"

"A paramour?" asked Justine stiffly. "I don't kid myself that she's remaining faithful to my son. Or perhaps she knew something about who killed Cornelius and was unwisely attempting to blackmail them. Considering she was murdered, that appears to be a valid supposition."

Burton made another few notes and then asked, in the same tone he'd used before, "Can you account for your actions last night and early this morning?"

Despite Burton's easy tone, Justine stiffened even more. "My actions? Surely, I'm not a suspect. I can assure you that flinging young women from decks is not in my wheelhouse."

"It's just a matter of protocol," said Burton with a small smile. But the smile didn't quite reach his eyes.

"Last night, I had dinner at my house with Nate."

For the first time, Justine seemed at a loss. She gave Burton a tight smile.

Burton asked, "Was Pearl there?"

"She was not."

Burton asked, "Was it common for you and your son to have dinner together without Pearl?"

Justine cleared her throat. "No. No, it wasn't common." She stared off toward the lake for a few moments and then added gruffly, "I know what this must look like, but I can confirm that Nate is a very easy-going man. He has many faults, mostly centered around his trusting nature. But he would never have harmed a hair on Pearl's head."

"They'd had a falling-out, then?" asked Burton gently.

Justine nodded. "Nate called me yesterday afternoon and said that Pearl had kicked him out of their house. Nate spent the night at my house last night. I can vouch that he was there."

Burton quirked an eyebrow. "You kept an eye on him the entire night?"

Justine snapped, "I'm a very light sleeper. I would definitely have been able to tell if Nate had left the house and started up the car. The driveway is right outside my window."

"Did Nate say what the argument was about?" asked Burton.

"There *was* no argument. Pearl simply got irritated with Nate and wanted him out of her sight for a while. It's very difficult for me to imagine. I can't see what Nate saw in that woman—she was as lazy as the day is long. You wouldn't believe the mess in their house. I know Nate should have helped clean up, but he was gone all day long and came home tired. You'd think Pearl would have taken some initiative to use a little elbow grease and get the place tidy. It wasn't as if she had a job and was working during the day. She wasn't even trying to find work."

Burton was happy to let Justine talk. He never gave the impression that he was annoyed in any way by her detour into the lack of cleanliness of the victim's abode. I figured he was always trying to let a person dig a hole for themselves.

Justine seemed to have realized that she was really denigrating Pearl for most of the conversation. "But even though I didn't always understand Pearl, I respected her and loved her like a daughter because she was important to Nate. Anything important to Nate is important to me."

"Of course it is," said Burton. "Out of curiosity, what will happen with Cornelius's construction firm now?"

Justine smiled at him, business face on. "Nate and I will take it over, naturally. I'm going to move Nate to the office side, too. I think that will work out best for him in the long run. I appreciate what Cornelius was trying to do to help out Nate, but I'm sure Nate doesn't really have a future on the building end of the business. I'm just delighted he's here in town and not over in Atlanta. I'll forever be grateful to Cornelius for giving him a start."

Burton tapped his pen on the notepad. "Do you have any further ideas now as to what is happening? It seems very unusual that there are two family-related deaths on the same property. Unless it's someone trying to send a message."

Justine gave an elegant shrug. "Perhaps it was Samson Green who killed Cornelius—I've mentioned that possibility before to you, Burton. I know he was unhappy with Cornelius for what he saw as a type of injustice. And maybe Pearl knew something and Samson felt he needed to get her out of the way before she spoke to the police."

"Did Pearl act as if she'd seen or heard something?"

Justine said, "Honestly, she could be a very secretive young woman. And she did drive around at all hours of the day and night, seeing these new friends of hers. Perhaps she saw someone arriving at or leaving Cornelius's house. Maybe she drove by to show off Cornelius's house to her friends and noticed that someone was there." A flash of irritation crossed her face. "But this is all really just conjecture, Burton."

A car pulled up and the driver's door flew open. Nate appeared, pale and sweating as he stumbled over.

"You called him," said Burton a bit grimly.

"I did." Justine lifted her chin. "He deserved to know, Burton. She was his girlfriend. And, no matter what I thought of Pearl, he thought the world of her."

I had the feeling Burton would have preferred to have spoken to Nate himself and perhaps seen and gauged his immediate reaction to the news.

Nate said in a halting voice, "Can I go inside? Can I see her?"

Burton's brows lifted up briefly. I realized that Nate didn't seem to know where Pearl's body was, if he was asking to go indoors. Of course, he could have deliberately asked the question that way to point suspicion away from himself.

Burton shook his head and said in a regretful tone, "I'm sorry, Nate, but that's not going to be possible. We have to protect the scene."

Just then a barrage of vans and cars approached.

"Excuse me for a second," said Burton. "I need to speak with the state police and the forensics team real quick."

Nate was looking very unwell and his mother started fussing over him. "For heaven's sake, Nate, take a seat. You look as if you're going to pass out on the sidewalk."

Nate didn't seem to be listening, so Justine gave him a shove and he plopped down on the driver's seat of Justine's vehicle.

"I just can't believe it," he muttered.

Justine strode over to the other side of her car and retrieved a water bottle. She gave it to Nate and commanded him to drink it. Obediently, he unscrewed the top and took a gulp and then another. Considering how much he was sweating, keeping him hydrated was a good idea.

"What happened?" he asked.

Justine explained why she and I were there and then said that I'd discovered Pearl below the deck. Nate looked a little green around the gills as he listened, his bloodshot gaze shifting from Justine to me and back again.

Nate frowned. "So—did she jump?"

Justine said sharply, "Can you imagine Pearl doing something like that? Of *course* she didn't jump."

It reminded me very much of Justine's reaction to the suggestion that Cornelius's death could have been an accident.

Nate said in a soft voice, "I just wondered . . . we'd had that fight and everything. I thought maybe she was upset about our arguing. Then her death, if she'd killed herself, would be all my fault."

"It would *not* make it your fault. And, as I said, it wasn't suicide or an accident. Pearl was murdered. So it's a good thing you spent the last night at my house."

Now a red flush started spreading in splotches over Nate's face. "You're thinking the cops believe I killed Pearl?"

"Well, of course they do. After all, however unwisely, you were in a relationship with her. The boyfriend is always a main suspect. Just keep that in mind as you're talking with them. Be guarded about what you say when they ask you questions." Justine frowned. "Maybe I should call Eugene."

"I don't need a lawyer, Mom."

"Lawyers protect the innocent as well as the guilty," said Justine briskly.

"Just the same, let's keep Eugene out of it, at least right now. I was home with you, anyway, so I have an alibi."

Nate looked completely miserable and totally exhausted. I wondered if he had gotten any sleep last night or if he'd stayed up worrying about his argument with Pearl.

Justine was thinking about the argument, too. "I think the *important* thing is to stress that you really didn't argue with Pearl."

"But that was the whole reason I was sleeping over at your place," said Nate dully.

"Yes, but you didn't argue. *Pearl* argued."

Nate wrinkled his brow as if trying to follow his mom's train of thought. "Well, I wouldn't really say she argued. She just wanted me out of there."

Justine said, "And maybe she completely manufactured your contretemps so that she could get you out of the way." She added impatiently as Nate didn't appear to follow her. "So that Pearl could come over here to Cornelius's house. I'm convinced she was here to scour the place for things to pawn. Apparently, she encountered someone else while she was here and they got rid of her so she couldn't say anything."

Nate turned and gave the house a sick look. "I never want to come over here again. Never."

"Don't worry, darling, we're going to sell the house as soon as possible. But listen—do you have any idea why Pearl wanted to come here? Do you think it's as I was saying . . . that she wanted to take a few things?"

Nate shook his head.

Justine pressed him again. "Pearl didn't mention wanting to get something out of Cornelius's house? Or that she was planning on meeting someone?"

"Mom, we really didn't talk at all after she blew up at me and basically evicted me from the house. I have no idea what she was doing here."

Justine pursed her lips. "She was up to no good, that's for sure."

Nate's sweet features were suddenly furious. "That's enough! I'm *sick* of you bad-mouthing her. All you did was find things about her to complain about. And when you talked to her, you were nothing but snide. You're the main reason she didn't feel welcomed by the family. At least Cornelius tried to get along with her."

Justine stiffened. "I always worked hard to ensure Pearl felt like a member of the family."

Nate gave a short laugh that sounded more like a sob. "Just get out of here, Mom. Go on, leave." He stumbled out of her front seat and took a few steps toward Burton.

Justine, apparently knowing when it was time to make an exit, quickly left.

Chapter Twelve

I SAID SOFTLY, "HEY, I'm so sorry about Pearl."

My attempt at kindness made him break down and he gave big wracking sobs while I delved with desperation in my purse for the errant pack of tissues I knew was in there. I finally found them and hastily proffered them to Nate. He took them gratefully.

Burton broke away from the state police and said, "Your mom leave?"

Nate said bitterly, "That's right. She wasn't helping, so I told her to just go home. You were done talking to her, weren't you?"

Burton nodded. "I know this has got to be hard on you right now. I'm sorry we have to go over this, but if we're going to find out who's responsible for Pearl's death, it's important that we start out on the right track as soon as possible."

Nate gave a last swipe of his eyes with the tissues and straightened a little. "Ask me whatever you want. I want you to find who did this."

"Can you tell me about the last time you saw Pearl and your movements from then until now?"

Nate took a deep breath. "Yeah. I came home from doing construction last night pretty late. Pearl was waiting for me. At first, I didn't realize anything was wrong, but then I saw that she'd packed an overnight bag for me, full of stuff."

Burton said, "Pearl wanted you to move out?"

"No. No, that's not what she said. I'd gotten the impression that she was mad at me about *something*, but she didn't want to hash it out. She said she just needed a break for a night or two . . . that she wanted a little space."

"Were you surprised by that?" asked Burton.

"Sure. I didn't know what I'd done. I was mentally trying to go through all kinds of stuff in my head—did I miss some sort of random anniversary? Did I screw something up . . . like drop the ball somehow? I tried to ask Pearl what she was upset about, but she just snapped at me and told me to get moving."

"And you did?" asked Burton.

"Of course. When Pearl wanted something, she usually found a way to make it happen."

Burton asked, "So you left your house and went where?"

"To my mom's." Nate shrugged. "She's always happy to see me, but she was pretty indignant that I had been basically thrown out by Pearl. She was in the mood to carp about Pearl the rest of the night, which I really didn't feel like listening to. I ended up heading to my old room after we ate dinner and just hung out there the rest of the night."

"You didn't see her the remainder of the evening?"

Nate seemed to realize his mistake too late. Now he'd pretty much upended any sort of alibi he and his mom had had. "No," he admitted.

Burton nodded again. "Okay. How about Pearl? Did you talk to her after you last saw her?"

"No. I tried calling and texting her, but she was ignoring me." He paled a little. "Wait. Do you think she was already dead when I was reaching out to her?"

Burton said smoothly, "I'm afraid that's something our team is going to have to determine later. As far as you know, has Pearl mentioned any issues with anyone? Any arguments or hard feelings? Is there anyone that you can think of who would have wanted to do away with her?"

Nate shook his head slowly. "No. She was just starting to make friends here and those women didn't exactly have deep relationships. They were just about going out and having fun together. This has to somehow be tied in with my uncle's death, doesn't it?"

"Do you think Pearl could have known something about Cornelius's death?"

Nate looked startled. "How could she? She wasn't even around him that night—she was out with those new friends I mentioned."

Burton asked, "Could she have driven past his house and seen something?"

Nate hesitated. "If she did, she sure didn't say anything to me about it." He paused, thinking for a few moments. "Although, I did feel a few times recently that there was something that maybe she was holding back."

"She was being secretive?"

"I wouldn't say *secretive*, but it was definitely like she had something on her mind that she didn't really want to share with me. I guess it could have been something about Cornelius. I thought maybe she wasn't really happy here and just was trying to give it a chance before she told me she didn't want to be in Whitby anymore." Nate shrugged. He added, "But if she did know something, that means she was trying to . . . what? Blackmail somebody?"

"Does that sound like something she might have done?"

Nate quickly said, "No. No way. Pearl wasn't involved in any shady stuff." But there had been another expression on his face before it was quickly replaced.

Burton said, "Circling back around to my question, can you think of anybody who might have done this?"

"Only if the killer knew what she'd found out and needed to get rid of her. So I guess it goes back to the original death, right? To my uncle's?"

Burton nodded. "In that scenario you've imagined, yes."

"I keep thinking about Samson. He was around a lot and my uncle kept saying he was trying to get in touch with him. Maybe Samson got frustrated and killed Cornelius and decided to do away with Pearl because he thought she knew something." Nate looked seriously at Burton. "Look, I know I'm probably a main suspect because I was in a relationship with Pearl. But I never would have touched a hair on her head. I *loved* Pearl and wanted to spend the rest of my life with her."

Nate's voice cracked a little at the end and he took a moment to regain his control. Then he continued, "I wanted to marry Pearl, but she wasn't quite ready yet. Please, find out who did this and don't waste any time looking at me—I didn't do it."

A few minutes later, Burton released Nate to return home. Nate slumped a little when he did, and I figured he was deciding whether he wanted to face going back to Pearl's and his house yet or whether he just wanted to head over to his mom's. His face reflected that confusion as he drove away.

Burton looked at me and gave me a wry look. "You know you could have left before now."

"It was never officially stated," I said with a small smile.

"I know you were interested in hearing all that and I can't really blame you. You've come over to this house twice to pick up books for the library and twice you've discovered bodies."

When he put it that way, it didn't just sound like a hardship—it sounded suspicious. "Yeah," I said, wincing. "Don't you have some questions you need to ask *me*?"

Burton gave me a weary grin. "Well, we had to officially consider you as a suspect because you were on the scene both times. But when the state police and I were chatting a few minutes ago, we could think of absolutely no reason why you'd commit these crimes. In fact, doing something to negatively impact library renovation would be the opposite of what you'd want."

"I'm relieved," I said with a smile. "And I'll admit that I did want to listen in to some of your conversation with Nate I really did like Cornelius and hate what happened to him. And then to Pearl, too, of course." I said the last in a less-convincing voice.

"So you weren't really a member of the Pearl fan club?" asked Burton.

"Not too much, no. I didn't have anything against her or anything, but I didn't get the best impression of Pearl when I'd spoken to her."

"And the family seemed like they weren't crazy about her, either." Burton quirked an eyebrow as if inviting me to offer thoughts on that.

"I think Pearl wasn't exactly who they wanted for Nate or thought he should be dating," I said. "Justine had really high expectations for Nate. I'm sure Pearl wasn't someone she'd have handpicked for him. She was sort of rough around the edges."

Burton nodded. "I got that impression too when I was talking to her. I also felt like she was holding something back."

"Hiding something?"

"Either hiding something or just trying not to share information she had."

I said, "I wonder if that contributed to her death."

Burton sighed. "It might have done so. At this point, I'll consider anything."

A few minutes later, I left to go to the library, book-free again. The whole way back, I was thinking about Pearl. Had Nate left Justine's house and followed Pearl to see what she was up to? Was she having an affair with somebody and was meeting him for some reason at Cornelius's house? Nate could have followed her, realized she was cheating on him, waited for the paramour to leave, seen red, pushed her off the deck, and then gone back to his mom's house, acting like nothing had ever happened. He sure *seemed* like he was being very open with Burton, though. He didn't have to mention the argument with Pearl. And he'd looked like he was really upset about Pearl's death.

Then there was Justine. She was definitely trying to make sure Nate wasn't considered a suspect, but her alibi for him wasn't going to be worth much. It wasn't like she'd kept her eyes on him the whole night in that big house. It would have been easy for Nate to escape from his mother's house without her hearing a thing, no matter how light a sleeper Justine was.

I didn't think Justine had liked Pearl at all. Would she have gotten *rid* of Pearl, however? I had a tough time picturing it. But what if Pearl knew that Nate had been involved in his uncle's death? Maybe Pearl had set up a time and place to meet with Justine and extort money from her in exchange for her silence. She sure wouldn't have tried to blackmail Nate . . . he didn't have the kind of money that his mother did. Justine didn't seem like the type of person who'd accept being blackmailed. I could totally see her pushing Pearl off the deck and then showing up here this morning to meet me for the books. Justine sure wouldn't tell Nate that she'd killed his girlfriend. He seemed to be crazy about her.

And then there was Samson. If Pearl did know something and was the blackmailing type, she easily could have coaxed him to come over. But Samson wouldn't have anything to pay her and he'd have known that blackmailing never really stopped. If he were desperate, couldn't he have killed Pearl to prevent himself from getting into an even bigger hole than he was already in?

There was Olivia, too. But I couldn't think why she might have murdered Cornelius since he operated mainly as her benefactor. He'd given her the house she lived in and seemed to try hard to find her better jobs, even though she'd later end up losing them. But I'm sure she would likely benefit from his will and maybe she was ready to be financially stable herself without the embarrassment of asking her big brother for help. Still, from what I'd been able to understand, she had an alibi. Samson had stopped by her house in search of Cornelius and verified she'd been ensconced with her cats at home.

Once I got to the library, I tried to switch completely into work mode since I knew I was going to have a busy day preparing for film club later in the morning. I wanted to let Wilson know about Pearl, but I saw he was on the phone in his office so figured I'd fill him in later. Luna came in a bit late, looking flustered, her mother in tow. "Is Wilson around?" she asked.

"He's in his office on the phone," I said with a smile. Wilson was a stickler for punctuality and Luna was a frequent offender for tardiness, although she tried doing better.

"I'll just slip in under the radar, then," she said with relief. Then she grimaced, glancing at her watch. "I've got storytime in five minutes."

Mona chuckled and shook her head as she watched Luna make her way through the bookcases to stay out of Wilson's view. "I swear I wasn't the one who made her late. That was all her own doing."

"I know you're always on time," I told her. "Luna's just not as much of a morning person, is she?"

"Goodness, no. But she does try. She laid out all of her clothes last night and even took her shower before she went to bed. But then she just dawdled instead of getting ready and then, when she finally got cranked up and going, it was already late."

"It happens," I said mildly. "Are you excited about film club today?"

Mona was hosting the club for the first time and I noticed she looked especially nice today with a blue, flowing top over white pants, a pearl necklace and matching earrings.

"I am and I'm so glad I settled on the movie I did."

I said, "I'm excited about seeing *Amélie* again. I'm looking forward to my armchair trip to Paris."

Mona said, "And it's a sweet movie, isn't it? My second choice was going to be very different."

"*Cool Hand Luke*?" I grinned at her. "That would have been starkly different in mood and tone."

"Yes, but I could watch Paul Newman all day long," said Mona with a dreamy sigh. "Although Wilson is also a catch."

We turned to look at Wilson through the office window. He was still on the phone, but gave us a confused smile, likely wondering why we were both staring at him. Mona gave him a little wave before trotting over to the periodicals section to do some knitting and occasional reading.

The next couple of hours flew by in a rush of patrons checking out books, a problem with the copy machine, and some research I was doing for someone. I glanced at the clock and realized it was about time for film club. I hurried to the community room, pulling out chairs and getting the popcorn machine ready to make the popcorn. I remembered I'd left the DVD in the car and headed out to the parking lot. While I was outside, I spotted Linus walking by with his dog, Ivy. Linus lived nearby and always took Ivy for a stroll at lunchtime. He hadn't seen me but Ivy, a large dog of indeterminate heritage and a sweet face, did and stopped still, wagging her tail. Linus followed her gaze and gave me a wave before walking over.

"Hi, Ann," he said with a smile. "Getting ready for film club, I'm guessing?"

I set down the DVD and stooped over to give Ivy some love. Her brown eyes shone up at me.

"You've pegged it," I said, grinning back at him. I hesitated and then asked, "Are you thinking about joining us after you take Ivy home?" I was careful not to be pushy—Linus was a major introvert and I didn't want to make him feel uncomfortable although I always wanted to make him feel welcome. His quick flush told me that he *wasn't* going to join us, but didn't mind being invited.

"Oh, not today, I don't think. But thank you, Ann." He cleared his throat. "I've noticed it's been very quiet in the library lately."

"Yes, the construction work is temporarily on hiatus, although I think they'll likely start back up soon." I sighed. "I hope they do, anyway. It's a double-edged sword, isn't it? The construction is noisy and disruptive, but it does need to be finished and things will be much better here when it is."

He nodded and said slowly, "I read in the paper about Cornelius Butler's death. I was sorry to hear about it. He was always very kind—he'd greet me every day."

"Isn't it awful? I'll miss seeing Cornelius here."

Linus said, "I may take advantage of the break in the construction, though. My friend Cecil is a chess player and has been wanting to have a game. Maybe we could have it here at the library. Even if it starts up again, the background noise helps me to focus, for some weird reason. It's almost like a white noise when the construction is going on."

"Sounds like a good plan since we don't know when the construction is going to start up again."

He nodded. "Well, I'll let you go get ready. See you in a little while."

I gave Ivy another goodbye rub and watched as she happily trotted off with Linus. Then I hurried back in with the DVD, and a few minutes later, the film club members started cheerfully filing into the room with Mona in the lead. George, a burly member who owned a typewriter repair shop, came in saying, "I almost thought I was in the wrong place! No construction is going on."

I grinned at him. "I know, isn't it great? Just in time for us to enjoy our movie."

Timothy, our youngest film club member and my helper during the technology drop-ins, came in and gave Mona a hug. "Looking forward to the movie."

Mona beamed at him. "How's my honorary grandson doing today?" Over the last few months of film club, Timothy and Mona had begun chatting a lot more. Timothy, despite being a teenager, was an old soul in a lot of ways. It was truly amazing how much the two had in common with each other.

"Oh, pretty good." He flushed. "I wanted to introduce you to somebody." He glanced around the room and then gestured to a shy-looking teenage girl who'd somehow slipped into the room under the radar. She came over, leaning forward a little so that her long brown hair partially hid her face.

"Goodness! Who's this pretty girl, then?" asked Mona, beaming at the two of them. "What a lovely surprise!"

The girl straightened a bit at the praise and smiled back at Mona. "I'm Molly. Timothy has said so many nice things about you."

"Well, I wish I could say the same in return, but he's kept you a secret, I'm afraid! But I'm so glad to meet you, Molly. Do you like films, too?"

Molly shyly nodded. "I do, but I mostly watch a lot of costume dramas. Timothy's trying to get me to broaden the types of movies I watch."

Costume dramas. It sounded like Molly was another old soul.

Timothy introduced me then and a few minutes later it was time for me to call film club to order. I thanked our visitors (there were a couple besides Molly) for coming and then gave the floor to Mona to talk about the movie for a minute before we started playing it. Wilson came in looking a bit harried and all business in his tie and button-down. But as soon as he spotted Mona and she smiled at him as she spoke about *Amélie*, I could see him soften as he smiled back. As soon as Mona finished talking about the film and the lights had been dimmed, I saw them sitting together, quietly holding hands. Timothy and Molly were doing the same thing. I reminded myself that I'd have to try to get Grayson to a film club meeting at some point.

This film had always both made me smile and touched my heart, so I sat back, watched and enjoyed all the feelings as it played. When it wrapped up, everyone gave an enthusiastic round of applause.

Mona applauded, too, as she walked to the front of the room again. "Wasn't that a marvelous film? And there are so many interesting bits of trivia about it. I found a few online that I wanted to share." She put on her reading glasses and got her papers organized as I quickly turned the lights back on. "For instance, the newsreel footage that's shown in the film is from the funeral of Sarah Bernhardt."

"The silent screen actress?" asked George with some interest. "And weren't we going to tackle some silent films?"

Timothy said, "Oh yeah! We could choose one of Sarah Bernhardt's."

"If we can find them," said George. "Otherwise, I'd be down to see some Buster Keaton or Charlie Chaplin."

I carefully redirected the group back to Mona so she could finish her presentation on the film, although she seemed to be caught up in the silent movie discussion. After she was finished, everyone applauded again and helped me clean up the room. Fitz made a guest appearance, which charmed everyone, especially Timothy's new girlfriend, who sat on the floor while Fitz sat in her lap and purred blissfully.

Chapter Thirteen

THE REST OF THE DAY was quiet but busy as I got a lot of work done on library projects since there weren't as many patrons there. The next few days were much the same, with the addition of the return of the construction din as the work started up again, making Wilson very pleased.

The day of Cornelius's funeral rolled around. Wilson had asked me to attend with him to represent the library. The funeral appeared to be a major event, as I guessed it might be. The service was held in the largest church in town and it was standing room only. There was a full choir, an orchestra, and Cornelius's coffin lying in state in the midst of it all. It had all the earmarks of a Justine-coordinated affair and she looked very pleased, despite her attempt at a somber expression. Nate was sitting next to Justine and looked pale and listless. Olivia's eyes were wide as if she needed them as fully open as possible to take everything in.

After the service was finished, there was a reception at the local country club. Like the service, no expenses were spared. There were buffet tables of food in chaffing dishes and what appeared to be country club staff standing stiffly behind the tables to serve the guests.

"This is quite the reception," murmured Wilson as we stood in line.

"And it looks as if they were prepared for a large number of people," I said. This was a good thing because, if anything, the crowd had grown. There were many people I'd never seen here in Whitby before, which indicated there must be a good number of friends and family from out of town.

"I wonder when they'll have the receiving line for the family?" said Wilson.

I recognized the look in his eye. He was going to try to anticipate when it was being formed so we could be among the first to go through.

"They look like they're settling down with plates at that large table," I pointed out.

The country club banquet room was full of flowers of all sorts. The tables were decked with white tablecloths and more flowers. After Wilson and I had filled our plates (I'll admit to having taken a fairly large portion since I figured it might be my best and biggest meal of the day), we sat down at a small round table near the family. Again, I suspected this was because Wilson wanted to be able to move into the receiving line as soon as it was formed.

A couple of moments later, I saw a familiar, beaming face looking down at us. "Hi there!" said Olivia. "May I sit here with the two of you?"

Wilson stood up courteously and I wondered if he might be about to make a small bow. He resisted the temptation and gestured to the empty seat. "We'd be delighted . . . as long as you're not sitting at the family's table?"

We glanced over and Justine was glaring directly at Olivia.

"If it's just the same, I think I'd rather sit with you. Justine is looking edgy today, isn't she? And I so often seem to end up on her bad side when she's like that."

So Olivia sat to join us, her plate piled high with several different types of pasta. She looked at me and smiled. "You saw all my cats, dear. I'm thinking I could ask the staff for a to-go box and pile it with that salmon and tuna I saw in the buffet line. They'll love it so much! They'll think it's Christmas morning."

A man brushed closely by Olivia's chair and she gave a jump and a little screech which startled both Wilson and me, as well as the man who was passing by her. She immediately put her hand over her mouth and blushed. "Goodness me. Oh, I'm so sorry."

"Are you alright?" I asked her with concern.

"I am, my dear, I am. Never you fear. I'm just extremely jumpy, that's all." She glanced around us and then leaned in close. "I've been seeing spirits, you see."

Wilson looked alarmed at this and gave me a glance, mutely asking me to handle the conversation. Or perhaps to wrangle it to something more manageable. But I couldn't just completely maneuver the topic to something else without addressing the subject. "Spirits?"

Olivia nodded. "That's right. Cornelius and Pearl. They've been showing up at my house and I'm not 100 percent sure they won't follow me around to other locations."

Wilson was looking decidedly uncomfortable now. But I couldn't leave it alone. "Are they . . . friendly-looking? Or do they look distressed?"

"They look like they're trying to impart some information to me. But when they try to speak to me, it's very garbled. It's all been most distressing. And they upset the kitties so much."

Wilson gave me a frown and I quickly latched onto a subject change. "And how are the kitties, Olivia? Are they doing all right?"

Olivia's face took on a fond expression. "The little darlings. Yes, they're doing very well." She dug into her pasta and smiled blissfully. "Really, this food is excellent. I'll have to ask Justine where she found it. Very tasty."

I glanced across the room and spotted Samson Green at the buffet line. I watched thoughtfully as he piled his plate with food. "Do you know Samson Green?" I asked, wondering if Olivia had also heard about his problems with her brother.

"Who, dear?"

"Samson Green. He was a former employee of your brother's. He's the one who knocked on your door looking for Cornelius that night. It seems he might have had some complaints from an injury on the job some time ago."

"Did he? How very awful. No, I don't know anything about him, I'm afraid. But I do remember him looking for Cornelius, of course."

This surprised me a little bit, but then maybe Cornelius hadn't actually spent all that much time with Olivia . . . enough to fill her in, anyway. Maybe he figured his philanthropic efforts were enough and he didn't pursue conversations with his sister.

I remembered when Olivia had come into the library that day and had quickly left again after spotting her brother there.

Olivia almost seemed to be reading her thoughts. "Sometimes families are tough on each other. Don't you think?"

Wilson was still focused on his plate. I said, "I'm sure they are. I don't have any family of my own anymore, so I can't really say for sure."

Olivia colored again. "Oh, mercy. I'm so sorry."

I gave her a smile. "Don't worry—it's been a long time."

"I guess what I'm trying to say is that Cornelius always looked out for me but maybe didn't completely fill me in on what was going on in *his* life. Which is sort of funny, thinking about it. I believe he knew just about everything going on in *my* life. He was involved a lot more in my business than I wanted, but he did everything out of a place of love and concern for my well-being. At least, that's what he said."

Wilson finally spoke up. "I'm sure he felt that way. He didn't seem much like a meddler."

Olivia chuckled. "Didn't he? I'm not so sure, Wilson. But I don't really want to speak ill of the dead, especially since they seem determined to visit me."

Wilson shifted uneasily in his chair.

Olivia continued, "And now we have poor Pearl. I feel so badly for the dear girl. And Nate seems beside himself, of course, absolutely beside himself. He cared so much for her. It was really quite touching. I wonder what he's going to do now."

I said, "Justine seemed to think that Nate was going to join her in running the construction business."

Olivia blinked at me. "Oh, I don't think so, do you, dear? I can't quite see that happening. I mean, I love Nate. And I do think he has his talents. But I certainly don't see him running a large business. I can see *Justine* doing it, though. No, I suppose Nate might end up back in Georgia again. It wouldn't surprise me at all. Too many sad memories here. And ghosts."

Wilson gave a shiver.

I said, "Do you have any thoughts on who might have done this to Pearl?"

"Burglars, I think, don't you?" Her wide eyes were vague. "Or someone who was on drugs or something."

Wilson said quickly, "I'm sure you're right."

Olivia ate quietly for a few moments before saying, "I just wish that Cornelius and Pearl wouldn't come visit me. It's not that I don't love *seeing* them, it's simply that I don't want to associate with them this way. I get the strangest sensation when I see them. It's sort of like when I'm gardening and I see a snake. You try to avoid it, don't you? But I can't seem to avoid Cornelius and Pearl. And they just look so pitiful."

Wilson cleared his throat. "I'm sure they must. Excuse me, please, while I go get a little bit more of the fruit salad." He left the table with an air of relief.

I gave Olivia a smile. "Well, I hope things start looking up for you soon. I know it's been a really stressful time for you."

She nodded solemnly, taking the last bite of pasta. "It has been." She glanced across at Justine again and I could see Justine's tight look of disapproval in return. Olivia sighed. "I know I need to spend some time with Justine, but she's just so judge-y. She thinks my life is a total disaster."

"You seem very happy with your life," I said in return. I noticed that Wilson deliberately found someone else to speak with near the buffet table.

"Oh, I'm happy, yes. I'm spending most of my time at home with my furry babies. But Justine doesn't see happiness as success. She thinks a successful life is one where you have a big important job and lots of money. Justine says that I've 'squandered my opportunities.' I guess I haven't lived my life the way she'd want me to, but it doesn't mean it hasn't been worthwhile. Maybe I haven't been able to hold down a job. Maybe Cornelius did have to jump in and help me sometimes. But he wanted to. Justine doesn't."

I'd thought Olivia would probably be provided for in Cornelius's will. Since he'd taken care of her in life, I figured he'd probably have provided for her in death, as well.

Olivia seemed to read my mind again. "You're probably wondering if I received anything from Cornelius's estate. I certainly *will*, but the will has to go through probate and Justine warned me very sternly that it can take some time. That it's not an *immediate* process. She told me I needed to find a job in the interim because she was not going to be giving me handouts."

"Where are you thinking about looking?" I asked.

Olivia sighed again. "It seems like I've had jobs all over town and that most people wouldn't want to rehire me. Sometimes I'm late. It's easy to oversleep, you know? And then sometimes things come up and I might leave a little early. You'd like to think that workplaces are flexible, but that's so often not the case, is it?"

I said, "Would you like me to take a look? We have some job-hunting resources at the library that might help."

Olivia's brow crinkled and I suddenly got the impression that maybe she wasn't all that interested in finding a job at all. Maybe she was just using unavailability of jobs as an excuse. "Would you, dear? That's very kind of you."

I continued with the charade that Olivia wanted to find work. "Do you have any office skills?"

"Office skills?"

"Things like typing, creating spreadsheets, working office equipment, that kind of thing?" I could tell by Olivia's expression that not only did she not know how to do those things, she wasn't altogether sure what they entailed. "That's okay," I said quickly.

"Maybe it's best if I just casually look around town again," said Olivia. "When I'm out running errands, I could ask around and see who's hiring."

"Of course," I said, realizing this casual hunt was likely not going to happen.

Olivia glanced across the room and hurriedly said, "It's been so very nice speaking with you, my dear. I'm going to go find a takeout box and get some fish for the kitties."

I turned to look in the direction Olivia had been gazing in and saw Justine coming toward us, looking irritated.

"Disappeared again," said Justine, making a huffing sound. "Unbelievable."

"Olivia, you mean?" I asked.

"She's been avoiding me," said Justine, taking Olivia's seat and drumming her fingers on the table.

I cleared my throat. "By the way, the funeral service was lovely. And I think the reception and the turnout is an amazing tribute to Cornelius. As I've said before, we'll all miss him at the library."

Justine gave a distracted *hmm*. Then she said, still apparently thinking about her sister, "What did Olivia talk with you about?"

"Oh, she was sorry about Pearl."

"Hmph. Did she mention looking for employment?" asked Justine.

I cleared my throat again, nervously. "She did a little, yes. She said she was going to look for a job while she was out running errands."

Justine gave a barking laugh. "Right. Because *that's* so effective."

I said, "I did extend an offer to her to help her use the library's resources to find work. And sometimes we have listings on our job board near the front door."

Justine said, "But that would make too much *sense* for Olivia to take you up on it. Olivia never does anything unless it's absurd." She drummed her fingers on the table again. "What kind of work do you usually see offered when you're helping patrons?"

"Well, it depends on what's available of course, but there's usually a motley assortment . . . some skilled labor, some office work, shift work. Some of it entails a drive to the next town over, but not all of them. I did ask Olivia if she had any office skills."

Justine snorted. "Olivia doesn't really have any marketable skills. That's the problem. Then she compounds that problem by not being considerate in terms of when she shows up and leaves."

I said slowly, "I know she loves animals. We could check and see if the county shelter needed any help."

Justine's eyes opened wide. "Oh no. Don't do that. Olivia would end up bringing more cats home. She'd never be able to avoid the temptation. It would be like putting a prescription drug addict to work in a pharmacy."

I thought Justine was being a little unfair to her sister, but I realized that Olivia's job problem had apparently been an ongoing issue and one that Justine clearly had little tolerance for.

I said, "She doesn't seem to be too worried, at any rate."

"Don't say that like it's a *good* thing. Olivia *should* be worried. She should be thinking about the fact that it's going to take a while for Cornelius's will to go through probate. What's she supposed to live on while that's happening?" Justine looked broodingly over at her sister who was beaming with delight at the food on the buffet table. "There isn't going to be a buffet every day for her to eat from. Really, I don't know how she does it."

We were quiet for a few moments and then I shifted the topic just a little. "How are things going with the construction business? I'm thinking that must be a very different type of work to step into after being a lawyer for so long."

Justine shrugged. "Not really. Half of law is just being organized. I have that down to a T. Cornelius did help a lot by having everything pretty tidy in the office and labeling folders. It's just a matter of management and I do have business skills." Her gaze shifted and her eyes narrowed in response. "What's *he* doing here?"

I looked over in the same direction. "Samson?" I asked.

"Yes. I can't believe he'd have the gall to be here. For all we know, he's the one who put Cornelius in that coffin to begin with."

I wasn't sure how to respond to that. I was still clearing my throat and searching my brain for an appropriate answer when Justine gave me a chilly smile. "Well, I should be speaking with others. See you soon, Ann."

Wilson was looking my way and gave me a small thumbs-up. I wasn't at all sure that my conversation with Justine was thumbs-up worthy, but was glad that Wilson seemed to think I was representing the library well.

I'm sure I lost whatever points I might have scored with Justine just seconds later when Samson came over to join me. "Hi there," he said in a soft voice. "Do you mind if I join you for a few minutes while I eat? It's tough to find a seat here."

Chapter Fourteen

"OF COURSE," I SAID. "Yes, the service and reception have been really well-attended."

Samson nodded solemnly. "You probably think it's weird that I'm here, don't you? Considering all the things I was telling you about Cornelius. But the truth is that I still had respect for the man and wanted to come to his service."

He ate quietly for a few minutes and then said slowly, "I was wondering if you could give me a little information about Pearl's death. I bought a paper and looked for a story about it, but the newspaper didn't have much to say."

I cleared my throat. "I think the police are trying to keep most of the details under wraps, what with the investigation and all."

Samson nodded again. "I can sure understand that. I just felt really bad about it. I felt bad about Cornelius, too, of course, but Pearl was a *young* person. I didn't know her, but I'd seen her with Nate around town." He took a bite of green bean casserole and swallowed it down before continuing. "The police have been asking me lots of questions about it."

"About Pearl?" I asked, frowning. "They think you had something to do with it?"

"Well, I know they don't have any evidence because I didn't do it. But yeah, I guess they have their suspicions. I've been trying to gather more information so I can prove my innocence."

I said, "Did you give the police an alibi for Pearl's death?"

I saw Justine give me a cold look from across the room that literally made me shiver. Apparently, she was none too pleased about my speaking with Samson. No wonder Olivia had been trying to escape her sister earlier. Justine's disapproval was palpable.

Samson shook his head sorrowfully. "Afraid not. But I told them I was in no physical condition to kill anybody. My back injury decided to flare up and I'd been lying in bed. Didn't realize I was going to need an alibi or I'd have invited somebody over as a witness."

"You seem to be better now," I said with a smile.

"Yep. Did my PT exercises as gently as I could. And I have some medicine I can take when it gets to be too bad." He paused and looked across the room. "Oops. Looks like Justine has me in her crosshairs. She's really shooting me the evil eye."

"You know Justine?" I asked.

"Only a little. I saw her from time to time when I was working for Cornelius. I don't think she ever noticed me then, though. The only reason she knows who I am now is because Cornelius told her about me trying to get in touch with him and because the police probably asked her about me." Samson's face was glum.

I said, "Do you have any ideas about what might have happened to Pearl?"

"Not really. I mean, I didn't know Pearl, but it sure seems like whoever killed Cornelius must have killed her, too. Otherwise, it doesn't make sense, does it? Couldn't be two killers running around a small town like Whitby. Got to be the same person." He shrugged. "Maybe it was Justine."

"What makes you think that?" I asked.

"Oh, I don't know anything, like I said. But I do know Justine didn't like Pearl one whit. She didn't think Justine was good enough for her son."

My face must have looked puzzled because he quickly added, "That's one thing about being invisible to people. They say all kinds of things around you. This was some time back—before Nate and Pearl even lost their jobs in Atlanta and moved to Whitby. I was waiting for Cornelius to give me some instructions on a job and I could hear Justine complaining to Cornelius about Pearl from inside his office. She kept saying that Pearl didn't have any education and hadn't come from a nice family . . . that kind of stuff."

It sounded a little like Justine was considering her legacy and her standing in the town. That would have been hard on Pearl, not to immediately feel accepted. But then, from what I could see, Pearl wasn't exactly the kind of person who made things easy on herself, either. And she might not really have put a lot of stock into what Justine thought.

Samson said, "I guess some people are just raised to be sorta snobby. But I didn't get that same vibe from Cornelius. I mean, I wasn't happy with how I was treated with my injury, but Cornelius never looked down on any of the folks who worked for him. He'd jump right in and get his hands dirty with a project if he felt like we needed a hand. He wasn't just sitting in his office all day."

He glanced over again and caught Justine's glare again and winced. "Anyway, I guess I should keep moving along. I signed the guest registry and paid my respects." He looked up again and saw Olivia staring in his direction this time and flushed. The guy just couldn't seem to catch a break. At least Olivia wasn't glaring at him like Justine was.

"I'll see you around, Samson," I said.

He gave me a genuinely happy smile. "Thanks for that."

As he walked away, Justine and Nate stood at the back of the room for people to speak with them. Olivia had wandered off on her own and was speaking to a few people while clutching her takeout box. Wilson gave me a look and we both hurried over to stand in the short line. When I got to Justine, she said, "I see that Samson approached you. Keep an eye out—that one is dangerous. I've even seen him lurking outside of Olivia's house. As if *Olivia* could help anyone get a job. Who knows what his agenda is?"

I was about to respond when Justine quickly greeted the next person in line.

Wilson and I walked back to the car. As he drove back to the library, he glanced over at me. "It looks like Justine was having some words with you."

I nodded. "She was warning me about Samson. She said he was dangerous."

Wilson sighed. "I suppose there really isn't a great alternative to Samson in Justine's mind, in terms of who murdered her brother. She must feel that it can't be one of the family, so she's latched onto him. I confess, I feel a bit sorry for him. It seems like he's trying to make an honest living, and no one is really giving him a chance." Wilson added, "Thanks for sitting with Olivia. I always want to be pleasant to the family but there's just something about Olivia that drives me a little crazy. I hope it wasn't too obvious when I left."

"I don't think she's the most intuitive person in the world," I said dryly. "She was just fine."

"Did she ever get off of her ghost topic?" asked Wilson.

"She did. Ultimately, I think she was trying to avoid Justine. Olivia has a completely different mindset toward working and what success means. I think success, for her, is spending a happy day surrounded by cats and drinking tea."

We reached the library and headed into the building. It took a few minutes for me to change gears and get my head totally in library mode, so I tried doing some rote shelving until I got into the swing of things again.

I walked through the periodicals area, putting away magazines that the patrons had left out. Linus gave me his shy smile. He had a neat stack of books beside him and appeared to be in his non-fiction section of his day now, judging from the biography he was holding.

"How was chess?" I asked him. I was glad to hear that he was getting out a little and that he had a friend. He spent so much time at the library that I figured a change of his routine would have to be a good thing.

"It was good," he said, looking happy. "I thought for a while that I was going to lose the game but then I rallied at the end." His expression grew more somber and he said quietly, "I saw in the newspaper about the young man's wife."

I nodded. "Pearl, Nate's girlfriend."

We were quiet for a moment. "That family is going through a lot right now," said Linus. He paused and then added, "I did see the sister out the other day while I was on my way to playing chess."

"Justine? The older sister?"

He shook his head. "It was the one that comes in the library to visit Fitz. I don't think her name is Justine."

"Oh, you mean Olivia."

Linus said, "I saw she was holding her husband's hand pretty tightly. Hopefully he can give her comfort through so much unhappiness."

My eyes widened a bit. "Olivia was with someone when you saw her?"

"They were hand in hand, although it was brief when she saw me looking her way," said Linus.

"That's interesting—Olivia actually isn't married. Out of curiosity, what did he look like?"

Linus looked regretful. "I'm sorry, I wasn't paying that much attention. I just saw she was with someone and that was it."

"Oh, no worries—it's good to hear that Olivia is seeing someone. I was just surprised to hear it, that's all. She seems so ensconced with her cats."

Linus smiled. "Speaking of cats, where is Fitz today?"

"Oh, there was a brilliant sunbeam on the floor of the break-room and so he's curled up in it for a while. I'll have to check on him in a few minutes and see if he wants to join everyone in the library. He doesn't like being antisocial for too long." I was relieved to shift the conversation over to another topic and we spent the next couple of minutes talking about Linus's dog Ivy and Fitz.

Then I hesitantly asked, "I did want to ask you something, actually. But before I do, I want you to know that you shouldn't feel obligated in any way. And if you don't want to do it, that's completely fine."

Linus blinked at me, looking owlish as usual in his large spectacles.

I winced. "Nothing to be alarmed about. But my friend, Grayson, is the newspaper editor. You might have seen the series of profiles he's doing on local people."

Linus nodded, looking a bit more relaxed at the more-familiar topic. He read the local paper daily, after all. "Yes. Local businessmen and politicians. A most-insightful series."

"That's right. He was thinking about expanding on that, as a matter of fact. He thought it might be interesting to include other local people—an assortment of folks. I suggested Mr. Trenton."

Linus quickly nodded again. "Our county refuse collector. Yes, he'd make a great choice. He and I have talked a couple of times since he's at the library fairly often."

Not nearly as often as Linus, though. "I also suggested that you might make a great choice, Linus. I know I'd like to find out a little more about you, at least."

A light pink flush suffused Linus's features at the idea. I quickly added, "Like I mentioned, there's absolutely no obligation to do that. And you could think about it. I just told Grayson I'd ask you about it."

"And . . . Grayson. He was interested in possibly speaking with me?" asked Linus slowly.

"Absolutely. Right away."

Linus considered this for a few moments, pushing his glasses up his nose. "I think . . . I think I might like that." It was as if he had to feel out the idea, carefully giving it consideration. He gave me a shy look. "Being part of the paper might be very pleasant."

He looked pleased, which made me smile in return. "I'm so glad. I'll let Grayson know. Maybe he can run by here after he finishes the story on Mr. Trenton and even speak with you here at the library."

I could tell that idea appealed to him. Being here at the library for the interview would give him sort of a home field advantage. And then, feeling he needed a break from conversation altogether, I left him with his books.

Back at the reference desk, I was trying to process what Linus had told me earlier about Olivia. He was nothing if not a trustworthy observer. But what did it mean? I was relieved when Burton walked into the library minutes later. He was carrying some books to return, but I had the feeling he was there to see Luna when he immediately looked for her over in the children's section. Not spotting her and looking a bit disappointed, he came over to the reference desk.

"Hey there," I said, "I'm glad to see you. How are things going with the case?"

Burton shook his head. "We haven't narrowed it down yet. We'll get there, but it's taking some time." He glanced across the library again. "Is Luna working here today?"

I hid a smile. "She is. We're fully staffed today, actually. She's probably finishing putting away the storytime props."

Burton suddenly looked decidedly more cheerful. And I didn't try to hide the smile anymore.

Fitz bounded up and wound himself around Burton's legs. He stooped down to say hi to him and Fitz lifted his chin for some scratches. "By the way," I said, "I wanted to let you know what a patron just told me a few minutes ago."

Burton listened as I filled him in on Olivia and her suitor. "And he said that they were definitely together as a couple?"

"That was his interpretation of what he saw. And he's one of those people I trust implicitly."

Burton rubbed the side of his face and considered this. "Okay. That's interesting, since she never mentioned she was seeing anyone, at least to me or the state police. Did she say anything to you about dating anybody?"

I shook my head. "No, and no one else mentioned it, either—and I spoke with everyone on behalf of the library. Maybe she's kept her relationship secret from her family. I have to wonder if maybe there's a quiet rebel vibe in Olivia. Maybe she's trying to prove her independence or saying to the family that she can't be manipulated or told what to do."

"But she *isn't* independent. She's been getting lots of help from the family to pay her bills or to find jobs."

I said with a shrug, "Maybe she and this guy just really hit it off and Olivia is trying to keep that under wraps. Maybe she thinks they'll disapprove of him for some reason, like they seemed to disapprove of Pearl."

Burton snorted. "Like successfully keeping a relationship under wraps happens in a small town very often." He glanced up and suddenly ran his hand over his hair to straighten it.

Sure enough, Luna walked up. She gave us a grin. "Okay, call me nosy. But I saw the two of you deep in conversation and I wanted to know what was up. How's the investigation going, Burton?"

"We're getting there, but we still don't have anyone in custody yet." Burton paused and looked to me for help. It wasn't like him to be tongue-tied, even around Luna, but he was giving every indication that he was.

I glanced over at the clock and said, "Luna, you never took your break this morning."

Luna chuckled, "Yeah, and I'm feeling it now. I had back-to-back storytimes."

"You know, the only way you're actually going to take a break is if somebody takes you out for coffee," I said.

Luna said, "Yeah, but you and I don't take breaks at the same time. I have a feeling Wilson would frown on that. Of course, Wilson frowns at a lot."

Burton cleared his throat. "Actually, I haven't taken a break, myself. I was going to head over to the coffeehouse to grab a muffin and a cup of coffee . . . want to head over there with me, Luna?"

Luna gave him a quizzical look and I thought for a moment that she was going to turn him down. But she looked at her watch and said, "You know, I think I could use a little pick-me-up before the high school kids come in for the program this afternoon. That sounds great. Let me just go grab my purse."

She hurried off and Burton gave me a smile. "Thanks, Ann."

"Sometimes we all need a little push," I said with a smile of my own.

When Luna came back after about twenty minutes, I casually asked, "How was your break?"

"Oh, it was pretty good. I had a vanilla chai latte at Keep Grounded. I love those things. I seriously think I could drink them all day long. And fortunately, it wasn't too busy in there. That place can get crazy, as you know. I had one of their vegan blueberry muffins and it was surprisingly good. Really moist and sweet and had just the barest hint of lemon."

Luna could be surprisingly unintuitive. I said, "Well, good. I'm glad the food and the coffee were good. How was the company, though?"

Luna wrinkled her brow. "What? You mean like how Keep Grounded is doing, business-wise?"

"No, I mean how was the company you kept? How was Burton?"

Luna's wrinkled brow deepened a little. "Well, he was Burton. You spoke to him, yourself a little while ago. He hasn't made a lot of progress with the case or anything, but he's plugging along."

I felt like I wanted to hit my head against the wall. "Luna, remember when I told you Burton really cared for you? I don't think that's changed."

"I know. I'm just not sure yet what I feel for him. And he's just so doggone patient. I don't feel like I really have to rush into anything. I've had a slew of bad relationships before and don't want another one. Plus, I'm so busy with the library and my mom."

"You don't have to get into a lifetime commitment. It's just coffee. Or going to a movie. Maybe just companionship."

"True. And Burton is easy to spend time with. He always seems very friendly and polite but not flirty."

"I don't think 'flirty' is in his wheelhouse. He always looks for you whenever he comes to the library. He's *at* the library a lot more than is warranted. Plus, he's really increased the amount he's reading and I don't think it's just because he's trying to research World War II. And think of all the nice things he does for you and your mom. He's run errands before and things like that."

Luna looked thoughtful. "That's all very true." She was quiet for a few moments. "He's a really sweet guy."

Uh-oh. That sounded like the kiss of death for any sort of budding relationship between the two of them.

Luna continued, "Like I said, I'm just not sure if I feel the same way."

I said, "That's what dating is all about . . . seeing if it goes anywhere. And it might not. If you had a nice time, why don't you follow up with him later? I know he's busy right now with the investigation, but maybe you can suggest another coffee together when you see him next time."

Luna nodded. "Maybe I'll do that."

Chapter Fifteen

A COUPLE OF DAYS WENT by. They were busy days with lots of patrons in the stacks, job hunters on the computers, and schoolkids doing homework and group projects after school. Fitz was delighted by the volume of patrons and also by the fact that the construction work that was now being done appeared to be in a quieter stage. He enjoyed lots of naps to catch up on the napping that hadn't happened during construction.

Sunday afternoon was the day of the festival that Grayson had invited me to. It was a warm day, so I dressed in shorts and a tee shirt. I took a string bag with a water bottle and a towel to sit on. Before I left, I made sure to put on some sunscreen so I wouldn't end up with a burn . . . it definitely didn't take much sun to scorch me with my coloring.

Grayson tapped on the kitchen door right around one p.m. I let him in and he gave me a big hug as Fitz wrapped himself around his leg.

"Is Fitz jealous?" asked Grayson with a chuckle as he stooped down to give Fitz attention.

"I think he's more jealous that I was getting your attention," I said, smiling at him. "He really likes you."

"Wish we could take you along, little guy," said Grayson. "But it's not really going to be the best kind of environment for a library cat."

A few minutes later, we got in the car and headed over to the park. The park itself was a beautiful place with views of the mountains as a backdrop. We lucked out on parking because someone left just as we got there. There were tons of cars there since people came from neighboring towns to attend and the festival was well-known because it had been going on for years. We got out of the car with our stuff. I could smell the food trucks and my stomach growled a little in response.

"Where do you want to start out first?" asked Grayson.

The festival, besides having arts and crafts on display and for sale, also had a couple of different stages featuring wildly different music. I'd looked at the schedule before we left, but everything sounded good.

"Honestly, I have no idea. Maybe it would be nice to start out with something more mellow and then work our way to something a little livelier. If we do mellow, then I'm torn between the jazz and the folk music stages. Any ideas?"

Grayson said, "How about if we go to the jazz stage first? There's a group there that I've listened to online before and they sound really good. And they're definitely mellow. Their songwriter is really good too, for the songs that have lyrics. Does that work?"

"I'm just glad to have some direction. Maybe after that we can walk around and take a look at some of the art. The crafts might be cool, too."

"Sure. Are you looking to buy anything?"

I shook my head. "With my budget, I'm just looking. But I love seeing all the different types of art. I especially wanted to see some of the glass that's for sale."

As we were walking in, my phone rang. I sighed. "Sorry." The last thing I wanted was to be interrupted when Grayson and I were actually going to spend some time together.

"Maybe you should check it," suggested Grayson.

I pulled my phone out of my pocket and looked at it. "Olivia," I said with a frown.

"Cornelius's sister?" asked Grayson in surprise.

"She has my cell phone number from when I was arranging food for her from the library. Maybe I should take this." I answered the phone. "Olivia? What can I help you with today?"

"Hi there, dear! Good to hear your voice, Ann. I was wondering if you had some particular books at the library for me."

"More regencies?" I asked.

"No, not this time. I'm looking for nonfiction, actually. Reference books on spiritual guidance."

"I'm actually not working today, but I can take a look when I'm at the library tomorrow. So you're looking for topics on mindfulness, maybe? Or perhaps something with a more religious aspect?" I asked.

Olivia gave her tittering laugh. "Sorry, dear. I'm doing such a bad job explaining this. And on your day off, too! I'm terribly sorry. Do you remember how I told you I'd been communing with my brother? And Pearl too, actually. They've been visiting me quite a bit."

"I do remember that, yes." It was hard to forget . . . or to forget Wilson's face when he listened to her at the funeral reception.

"Well, I thought I might fine-tune my communications." Olivia's voice sounded excited. "Our conversations seem sort of mundane right now."

I hesitated, not really sure I wanted to ask the question. Curiosity won out, however. "What kinds of things are you talking about?"

Grayson quirked his eyebrows at me and I grimaced.

Olivia said brightly, "Oh, the silliest things, but just what you'd expect. Cornelius is still after me to find gainful employment. He seems to think they're hiring at the ice cream shop. But who wants to work with a bunch of teenagers? Not me! And then Pearl, she's grumbling over Nate still. I'm not completely sure she realizes she's dead at all. Instead of all this nonsense, I thought I might be able to have more productive conversation. Perhaps on who killed them? I think that's pertinent, don't you?"

She seemed to be waiting for an answer. I said slowly, "I would think so, yes. But Olivia, I'm not absolutely sure there are books about channeling those sorts of communications at the Whitby library. I could take a look, though, and see if there's anything I can find for you in interlibrary loans."

"Would you? What a dear you are. And on my end, I'll keep you updated on my investigation. Ta-ta!" And with that, she was gone.

Grayson's eyes crinkled. "That sounded like a fascinating discussion."

I chuckled. "Never a dull day at the library. Even when I'm away from the library."

We lay down a couple of old blankets from our bags and sat where we could watch the musicians. Grayson was right—they were excellent. I loved watching them almost as much as I enjoyed listening to the jazz. They alternated their songs between relaxing and a little more energetic. We pulled out water bottles and pimento cheese sandwiches that Grayson had packed and enjoyed the warmth of the sun and the light breeze that complemented it.

The group took a break and while they did, Grayson and I lay back on the blankets, drowsy from the sun and the food. Then his phone rang.

"Argh," I murmured. "What sadist is calling you on a Sunday afternoon during a festival? Olivia? Has she decided to tell the newspaper about her ghostly visits?"

"It's Zelda Smith," said Grayson with a sigh.

I groaned again. "Surely there can't be any homeowner association tasks today. No one could be in the process of painting their house purple or asking for permission to put up a ten-foot fence. Everybody in town is here."

Grayson answered the phone with a remarkable amount of cheerfulness in his voice. "Hi there, Zelda."

I couldn't make out the words on the other end of the line, but I could definitely hear the dark mutterings that indicated Zelda was displeased with something.

"Oh, I don't think they need an answer back on their architectural review *today*, Zelda. You're saying they just emailed it to you?"

I looked up at the sky and watched the puffy clouds morph into various animals and shapes and then back into amorphous clouds again. Grayson had a lot more patience than I did with Zelda. It was funny, because I was always very patient at the library with all my patrons, even the ones who were real challenges. But maybe it was harder for me when I was off work. Maybe I used up all my patience at the library, or most of it.

Grayson was still listening to Zelda as the jazz band started tuning up again after their break. "Do you like music, Zelda?"

There was a break in the dark mutterings on the other end and then a hesitant, questioning series of sounds.

"Well, why don't you meet Ann and me at the park? The art and music festival is going on and there's lots to see and do. We don't have any plans—we're just wandering around."

There was another pause on the other end and then a short reply.

"Good. Give us a call when you arrive and we'll meet up with you." Grayson listened again for a moment and said, "Yes, maybe bring some water and a snack. Ann and I have blankets to sit on—if those work for you."

He hung up and gave me an apologetic smile. "Sorry about that. She just sounded so unhappy and grumpy."

Although the description of Zelda's current state of mind gave me pause, I smiled back at him. "That was really sweet of you. And you were totally right to invite her. I haven't really thought about it before, but her constant crankiness tells me that she needs something to do. She just seems really unhappy."

Grayson sat up, wrapping his arms around his knees. "That's what I was thinking. Whenever I speak to her, she's not in a great place. Maybe she just needs some time outside of her house. Maybe she's lonely."

I nodded and said wryly, "Unfortunately, I've spent most of my time trying to avoid her so I never picked up on that. I hope she'll enjoy the festival." Because, if she didn't, this afternoon was definitely going to go in a bad direction.

A few minutes later, Grayson said with surprise, "Oh, looks like Burton's here."

I followed his gaze and saw Burton walking in our direction.

"He's probably working the festival since there isn't much of a police department here in town."

"Even with a murder investigation?"

I shrugged. "The state police are still working it this afternoon, I'm sure. But the state police wouldn't be working the festival so he probably has to cover where he can."

"And look," said Grayson with a smile. "There's Luna and her mom."

Sure enough, Luna and Mona were haphazardly making their way around chairs and blankets and also moving in our direction.

"I did sort of finagle a coffee with Burton and Luna," I said. "Despite all the times people tried to set me up on horrific dates."

"How did it go?" murmured Grayson as both Burton and Luna came within earshot.

"Jury's out on that," I said.

Luna and Mona, who'd been entirely focused on not tripping on their way over, finally spotted Burton with surprise. "Well, look who's here," said Mona, beaming.

Luna looked a bit more flustered. I wondered if she was thinking of my advice to her to ask Burton out for a coffee the next time and just see where things led.

"How's it going, Burton?" asked Grayson.

Burton smiled at us all, although I noticed an especially tender look for Luna. "Pretty good, pretty good. I had to step in to help out with the festival for a while so I got to hear some good music while I did. Nice break." He gave Luna a tentative smile again. "How are you enjoying things?"

"We've really liked it, but Mom thinks she might have gotten enough sun, so we're going to call it quits for today," said Luna.

"It's deceptively hot, too," said Mona, sighing. "I should have brought my hat. I *thought* about it, but I just didn't bring it."

Burton quickly said, "My shift is over and I've got to head back out to meet up with the state police. I could drop you by your house, Mona."

Mona quickly said, "Would you? That would be so sweet of you. I hated having to make Luna leave early because she loves the music and art here." She turned to her daughter. "Does that work?"

Luna said hesitantly, "Sure, if that's okay with Burton." I saw her take his hand and squeeze it really quickly. "Thanks so much."

Burton stood a little taller as he took Mona's tote bag and blanket from her and ushered her to his car.

"That was really nice of him," I said pointedly as we watched them walk away.

Luna gave a bit of a breathless laugh. "Yeah. Yeah, it was." Then, apparently not wanting to dwell on it for long, she said, "Okay, I'm going to take off and see that experimental group that's about to start playing. You two want to come?"

"That sounds like something you'll enjoy more than I would," I said with a chuckle. "It's all yours."

We listened to the jazz group again until Grayson got a call from Zelda that she'd arrived. We packed up our stuff and joined her. I could tell that Zelda had taken particular pains with her appearance, pulling back her henna-colored red hair into a loose bun. She was also wearing a black knee-length dress. I could tell that she was a little uncomfortable, a little anxious, about doing something completely different.

Grayson and I tried to put her at ease. He grinned at her and said, "Glad you could join us, Zelda!"

She gave me an apologetic look. "I hope I'm not intruding."

"The more, the merrier," I said warmly. I was surprised to realize that it was the truth. After all, if I'd wanted a private date with Grayson, we should have gone somewhere else.

Zelda was glancing around, taking everything in and looking just slightly overwhelmed. But then, everything that I'd ever noticed her doing was home-based. Her biggest commitment and community involvement was the homeowner association. She didn't venture out of the neighborhood much.

Grayson said, "Have you eaten yet?"

Zelda said, "Not yet. After I spoke to you, I got ready right away. Have you eaten?"

Grayson said, "We just had a little food that we'd brought but I wanted to introduce Ann to the food trucks that came in. Would you like to check them out?"

Zelda did want to. So Grayson took us over to an area of the park where there were a series of food trucks. Whitby was such a small town that we didn't ordinarily have food trucks here—these had traveled in for the occasion. And boy, the aroma coming out of these trucks made my mouth water, even though I'd already eaten a sandwich not too long ago. I'd thought Grayson was just being polite and trying to get Zelda some lunch, but as soon as I smelled that food, I was glad he'd brought us over there. There was one that was Mexican food, one that was Greek fusion, one that served seafood. The food options in Whitby had suddenly multiplied.

I ordered some street tacos and waited off to the side while Grayson patiently took Zelda on a tour of the possibilities. She seemed to be having a hard time making up her mind. Considering the choices, I could understand.

I heard someone call out my name and turned to see Nate there. He was looking a little better than the last time I'd seen him.

"Hi Nate," I said. "Good to see you here."

He smiled at me. "It was my mom's idea. Of course . . . she's always got ideas."

I spotted Justine off a little bit from us, speaking with a group of women. But she was keeping an eagle eye on Nate. She gave me a curt nod when she saw me looking in her direction.

"To be perfectly honest, I'm getting kind of tired of my mother's plans. And Whitby, too."

I nodded. "Small towns aren't for everybody. Especially if you've been used to being in Atlanta. I'd think it would be a tough adjustment."

"Honestly, it's a great little town. It's just too small for both my mother and me to coexist in. Plus, it's full of a lot of memories I'd like to get rid of." He sighed and rubbed his face. "I haven't told her yet, but a friend of mine in Georgia is planning on hiring me."

"Congratulations! Are you going to be doing real estate again?"

Nate shook his head. "Not this time. The economy has just been too unstable for me to feel comfortable with that career. I'm going to pursue a job in IT."

I raised my eyebrows. "Really? That's great. I didn't know you were so good at computers."

He gave a rueful smile. "That's the thing—I'm really not. I mean, I'm not *awful* with them, and I've always had an interest in computers. But my friend tells me this job is really low-key and would give me plenty of time to learn the ropes."

"Maybe you should run by the library tomorrow. We have tons of books on all different kinds of computer-related jobs. I'm sure we could find something there to give you an overview."

Nate's face brightened. "That'd be great. I was looking at buying something online, but I didn't really even know what to look for. Having a little direction would help."

"That's a big part of my job," I said with a smile. "And I think it's really brave of you to step away and try something different."

He said a little hesitantly, "Well, I got a little braver when I realized I have a safety net. When my uncle hired me on as an apprentice, he let me buy a percentage of his construction company. When his will was read, I found out that any remaining interest in the company goes to me."

"Wow, that's great, Nate! That should make the whole process a little less stressful."

Nate choked up a little for a second then said, "Cornelius was always looking out for the family. He didn't leave my mom out, either. She'll inherit his retirement account. The only problem with me getting the interest in the company was that it sure made me look like the primary suspect," said Nate ruefully. "And I feel sort of bad since I'm not even going to be keeping an eye on the company at all. But I'm sure my mom will step in to do that."

He glanced back over at his mom with a brooding look. "She just doesn't want to talk about Pearl at all. The problem is, I don't really have anyone to talk to in this town. That's another reason I want to move."

I said, "I'm sure it would probably help you out to have someone to talk things over with. It's got to be so hard going through this alone."

"That's the thing. It feels like I'm alone, even though I have family around me. But they never liked Pearl and now they totally want to forget her and pretend she never existed. The problem is that I *want* to talk about her. The more I talk about Pearl, the better off I feel. And I want to do everything I can to figure out who did this to her."

His eyes narrowed and for the first time I could see a darkness in Nate. Before, he'd always sort of seemed like a happy-go-lucky guy to me. Not now. Pearl's death had somehow given him a purpose. She was motivating him more now that she was gone than she'd been able to when she was alive.

I glanced over at Justine, who appeared to be trying to break away from the group she was speaking to. "Any ideas?" I asked quickly.

He said, "I don't know. I just keep coming back to the idea that Pearl knew something. She must have seen or heard something the night she was out with her friends."

I nodded, but already felt a little disappointed. It sounded like Nate just wanted to have an epiphany, but the epiphany hadn't happened yet.

He added, "I just don't know what it is."

"She didn't say anything to you about it when she got back home that night?"

He shook his head. "Here's the problem . . . I wasn't actually there at home that night. We'd had *another* fight. Pearl had kicked me out again. When I called her the next morning, she was acting really remote. I figured she was acting that way because she was still mad at me for whatever stupid thing we'd been fighting about, but now I'm thinking she was just distracted because of what she'd seen or heard."

I wondered if Burton realized that Nate's alibi for Cornelius's death wasn't true. "What did you do that night?"

He shrugged. "I just drove around. I went to a bar, solo. It was lots of fun."

"Well, hello there, Ann," said a smooth, chilly voice.

Chapter Sixteen

I TURNED TO SEE JUSTINE standing right behind us. There was a tight smile on her face.

"Hi there," I said. "Are you enjoying the festival?"

Justine nodded stiffly. "It's a beautiful day for it. I remember last year it was stormy, but we lucked out this year. I'm actually on the planning committee."

Of course she was. Justine was nothing if involved in nearly every aspect of the town. It was a wonder that she wasn't on the library board. I suppose she figured that Cornelius had it covered.

Justine turned to Nate. "I was thinking we should head over and get a spot at the main stage before there aren't places there. You know how popular The Creek is."

"Sure," said Nate, picking up their bags.

"I'll talk to you later, Ann," said Justine.

It almost sounded like a threat. That was one tightly wound woman.

As they walked away, Grayson and Zelda joined me. Zelda had finally decided on a Greek gyro with lamb, tomatoes and onions. I had to admit it smelled delicious. Grayson had gotten a vegetarian pita for himself, which smelled equally good.

We decided it would be easier to listen to music while we ate instead of looking at the art, so we settled down in front of the main stage where The Creek, a popular folk band with a crossover hit, was playing. Like Justine had said, it was crowded with people there, but we found a spot under a tree to put our blankets down. Zelda had brought a small, folding chair, declaring herself past the point of sitting on the ground. She looked very content with her gyro and was tapping her foot on the ground in time with the music.

After the band finished, we strolled through the arts and crafts display. Zelda was especially interested in a pottery booth and found a few things there. I admired a vase and she insisted on buying it for me, which made me blush and bluster that there was no need to do that.

"Don't be silly," she said crisply. "We all need some random pretty things in our lives. Just be sure to fill it with flowers from your garden." She paused and then levelled me with a serious look. "You know, I thought your aunt was wonderful. And she was such a fantastic gardener. I'm glad to see that you're keeping up with the yard so well."

I'd inherited the house and property from my aunt, who raised me from a young age. She'd been a huge influence on me in many ways—one of the things she'd passed along was a love of taking care of a yard and the flowers and birds that inhabited it. I nodded to Zelda and said, "Thank you. And don't worry—I'll continue keeping up with it. It's one of the best ways to de-stress when I'm done with my day."

Zelda considered this thoughtfully. "But you enjoy working at the library, don't you? I know all the times I've walked by your yard and you've been sitting outside with a book in your hand. She's quite the reader, isn't she?" She asked this of Grayson.

Grayson said solemnly, "She's one of the biggest readers I know."

I remembered all the times Zelda had pushed me to be on the homeowner association board for our neighborhood. I kept telling her, very sincerely, that I just didn't have the time for it and the message never seemed to sink in. Maybe it was because Zelda thought I was enjoying every minute of my day at the library and came home rejuvenated. Which wasn't always the case.

I smiled at her and said, "I love reading. But working at the library doesn't give me too many chances to do that. I find the job really satisfying, but when you're working with the public, you never know exactly what you're going to get from day to day."

"So it can be exciting?" Zelda's face wrinkled into one big frown. I couldn't tell if she was disagreeing with the library being exciting as a fundamental principle, or whether she was just trying to wrap her head around the concept.

"It can be. On a very small scale."

Grayson said, "Every time I go in there, the place is hopping, Zelda. You see people from all walks of life."

We walked on through the booths, looking at the glass, the clothing, and the jewelry. I was surprised when Zelda commented again on the topic. "Does the library use volunteers or just paid staff?"

Grayson gave me a small, rueful smile. I know he was thinking that he'd gotten me into something of a jam. Would I want to spend more time with Zelda after spending a good deal of my adult life trying to avoid her?

But the truth was, the library could always use volunteers. We really treasured them. And, if there was one thing I knew about Zelda, it was that she was dedicated. I said, "We love our volunteers at the library. If you'd be interested just show up anytime and I can walk you through the process of becoming one."

Zelda quickly said, "But I'm not a reader."

I hid a smile. Zelda always told me that and I did remember. "It doesn't matter. If someone asks you for advice on a book, just send them my way and I can help them."

This seemed to satisfy Zelda and she gave a bob of her head, indicating that was the end of the matter.

We were on our way to listen to another group that Grayson enjoyed when Zelda spotted some older ladies from our neighborhood. "All right," she said gruffly, "I'm going to leave you two kids alone now. I see some folks I should catch up with. Thanks for inviting me along."

She hurried off to join her friends. Surprisingly, I wasn't as relieved as I'd thought I might be.

"She's not so bad, once you get to know her," said Grayson, echoing my thoughts. And we spent the rest of the afternoon listening to music and half-dozing off in the sun.

The next morning, I was at the circulation desk when Zelda showed up bright and early. I shouldn't have been as surprised as I was . . . Zelda was nothing if not focused and efficient. She

was dressed in black slacks and a black top and had taken it upon herself to wear a nametag.

"Good morning!" I said cheerfully. "Thank you so much for
coming in today to help out. We really appreciate it."

Zelda gave a stiff nod in response. "What do you need getting done today?"

This was the part I always hated. I felt like a lot of our volunteers really loved books and really loved people. But the biggest
need I had that day, and the biggest need the library had *most*
days, was for books to be shelved. These were books from the
book return drop and books that had been leafed through and
left out in various parts of the library.

"Don't sugarcoat it," said Zelda crisply. "I'm not here to dil-
ly-dally around. I like to get my hands dirty. If I'm going to volunteer, I want to be used and I want to be helpful."

"That's very generous of you," I said, meaning it. "I wish our
biggest need was more interesting, but right now it's shelving.
Let me give you a tour of the library and then I'll show you how
we do shelving here."

I gave her the volunteer tour, showing her the library (she
wasn't familiar with it at all—she was right, she was a non-
reader), pointing out the breakroom and giving her a card to
swipe herself in (although she sniffed at the idea of taking a
break), and showed her how the copier worked since patrons often needed help with it. Through the entire time, Zelda didn't
ask any questions or say a word, just nodded at the appropriate
intervals.

I walked her through shelving, showed her the carts full
of books, and said, "Shelving books can be a slog, so just stop

whenever you're ready. Again, we really appreciate the help because it frees us to do other things."

"It's my pleasure," said Zelda, although the expression on her face certainly didn't indicate that was the case.

I settled at the reference desk to work on helping a local college student find research materials for a paper he was writing. Then Wilson came up to me, a thoughtful expression on his face. "Ann, I was thinking we needed to try something different at the next weekly staff meeting."

I dearly hoped that he was going to say that he was going to completely discontinue the weekly staff meetings in favor of a nicely detailed email. That, however, didn't appear to be in the cards.

"What type of thing?"

Wilson said, "I think we should try an icebreaker."

My brow crinkled. "Is there ice that needs breaking?" The staff meetings always seemed rather congenial to me. The only thing that wasn't pleasant about them was the fact that we had them every week without fail, whether there was something to discuss or not.

Wilson sighed. "Not particularly, but the trustees think it would be a good idea. They think if the meetings are more relaxed, the staff might feel more comfortable about broaching concerns or asking questions."

"What type of icebreaker were you thinking about?"

I should have known what was coming.

Wilson said, "That's what I need you to figure out and implement. Maybe we can make it a recurring feature if it ends up going well."

His cell phone started ringing and he quickly answered it, rushing back to his office. I took a deep breath and delved into the world of icebreakers. I got into a lot of corporate examples online, which provided a rabbit hole that offered a lot of really wince-worthy ideas. I finally settled on something fairly innocuous—staff trivia. Then I fell down yet another rabbit hole as I tried to figure out fun but not invasive questions. I'd just have everyone email me their answers and then everyone would try and guess at the staff meeting who said what.

I glanced up a couple of times as I worked my way through the trivia stuff. I checked my phone once and groaned as I saw I'd missed a call from Grayson. We'd just not been in synch at all lately. I took a quick break to call him back. I called him and he picked up. "Hey there. How are you?"

I could tell from his voice that he must be in the middle of something. "Sorry—are you busy?"

"I am, actually. Can I catch up with you later?"

"Sure," I said. Before I could say anything else, he was gone.

I frowned. I wasn't going to obsess over this or anything, but we'd had a lot of near-misses lately on both of our ends. Grayson himself had labeled our lack of time together a problem. I didn't want to let it become more of one. I slowly walked out of the breakroom and over to the reference desk.

Zelda seemed to be taking pains not to disturb me. When a patron asked her a question, she actually appeared to try to figure out where the book was located, herself. She looked so grimly unapproachable that it was hard to imagine anyone seeking her out. I wasn't at all sure she was enjoying herself.

I moved on from the staff trivia back to the research for the student who'd emailed me. I was deep into that when I heard someone say my name and looked up to see Connor standing there. I groaned inwardly. Advice to the lovelorn was not my forte and I didn't really have the time today to be dealing with his personal problems. "Hey there, Connor," I said as amiably as I could. I saw Wilson glowering at his nephew from his office.

"Ann, I'm glad you're here. Can you take a break for a few minutes? I had something I wanted to run by you." He gave me a charming, pleading look.

I glanced at the clock. "It's not my breaktime yet. But what do you have going on? I can talk for a few minutes."

Connor said, "I'm here, as usual, for your priceless advice, my friend. I'm really in a jam this time."

I reflected that Connor needed to find more friends. Perhaps guy friends. And that I was happy once again that we were no longer dating.

"What's up?"

He plunged right in. "So I decided to stop trying to date Victoria—she's my coworker, the one I was telling you about. I didn't want to create any weird work vibes or make it seem like I was pressuring somebody there. That would really be an HR problem, wouldn't it? I met somebody when I was at the festival . . . her name is Cindy. We hung out for a while there and had a great time—music, food, art . . . did you go?"

I nodded and Connor continued, "Anyway, I made plans with her for Saturday night. But then Victoria came by to see me during my shift and invited me to her parents' 50th anniversary party."

I raised my eyebrows. "And that party is Saturday night?"

"Exactly. And Victoria didn't just invite me as a guest, she invited me to be her date for the event."

"It seems like really short notice to invite someone to a big party like that," I noted.

Connor shrugged. "Maybe it's not that much of a big party. Maybe it's a backyard barbeque or something more casual. But what do you think? Should I give Cindy an excuse and go with Victoria? Cindy and I don't have nearly as much in common as Victoria and I do."

"Young man!"

The peremptory voice, ruined by decades of smoking, rang out like a shot. Zelda, pushing the library cart full of books to be shelved, stared grimly at Connor.

"Can't you see that Ann is very busy with library work? Jobs are important things and she needs to get back to hers."

Connor was momentarily speechless from surprise but managed to regain his composure. "I'm sorry. I wasn't trying to get Ann into any trouble." He must have wondered who on earth this woman was, since he knew his uncle was the director of the library.

Zelda sniffed. "Perhaps if you had a job of your own, you'd understand a bit better."

"I'm a doctor," offered Connor.

Zelda did not appear to be impressed by this a whit. "Then you should be with patients right now instead of talking about your love life. And I've got your answer for you—keep your date with Cindy and tell Victoria that you had a long-standing obligation. If she's worth anything, she'll understand."

She gave another sniff and walked away, pushing the cart.

I gave Connor a rueful look. "She's not wrong, though, Connor. Cindy doesn't deserve to be dumped for Victoria. You could tell Victoria that you can't make it and then ask her if she'd go to something else with you instead."

Connor sighed. "Yeah, you're right. I guess I was just hoping to hear different advice. Now I've got the same advice from two different people." He frowned bemusedly at Zelda who, feeling his gaze on her, quickly turned around and glared at him. He reddened and looked away.

I said, "Sorry. Hey, let's catch up soon over coffee, okay? I'm going to be off some next week. Let me know what your schedule looks like."

He gave me a crooked smile. "Sure. Thanks, Ann. Sorry about disturbing you at work . . . again." He chuckled. "Looks like I'm getting the evil eye from my uncle, too, so I'd better hit the road."

The rest of the day was busy but well-paced at the same time. I got a lot of stuff knocked out that I needed to plan and helped a few patrons along the way. I finished my library column for Grayson, too. I was about to email it over to him when I glanced up and saw he was standing right in front of me.

"Hi there," he said with a grin. "Sorry, I didn't mean to startle you."

"Oh, I was just focusing on sending you an email with the column and you magically appeared. By the way, you'll never guess who was here first thing this morning."

"Zelda?" asked Grayson in the tone of one who was hazarding a stab at it.

I blinked at him. "Or maybe you *would* guess."

"When I was driving past the library earlier on my way to the office, I noticed her car out front. I knew she couldn't possibly be reading, so I figured she'd decided to start volunteering right away. How did she do?"

I said, "I never thought I'd be complimenting Zelda on anything, but she's actually a really fantastic volunteer. She did some shelving, tidied up the children's area, and even was good on a computer—Wilson had her entering new patrons into the database. She was very focused and diligent."

"And cheerful?" asked Grayson, a smile tugging at his lips.

"Don't be silly. Zelda's never cheerful." I grinned back at him.

"Hey, by the way, thanks for the tip on John Trenton. He was great to interview," said Grayson.

"Right? Super-nice guy and very entrepreneurial. He left a decent job to start his own business. You wouldn't think that trash collection would be such a great line of work to be in, but he seems to have done very well for himself."

Grayson nodded. "He took some risks at the beginning and made them work out. He couldn't qualify for a loan, so he leased some equipment until he was in a position to get loans or to buy outright. And he's turned it into a family business. His wife keeps the books, his son helps him collect the garbage. And his daughter keeps up his web presence and social media so that potential customers in the county can find him. Really interesting guy." He glanced across the library, squinting his eyes a little. "Were you able to broach the subject with Linus?"

"He looked really pleased to be asked and I think he *might* be interested. I left it where he could think about it and let me know so I wouldn't make him feel any pressure or anything. And I thought the interview, if it happens, should be here at the library so that Linus gets confidence from a home field advantage." I stopped short because Linus started heading our way. "Actually, I think he's coming over right now."

Linus hesitated before coming all the way up to us. "Am I interrupting anything?"

"Not at all," I said with a cheerful smile. "How are things going today, Linus?"

"Very good. I made a copy of the *New York Times* crossword and finished it in thirty minutes." He gave me a shy look.

"Linus, that's fabulous. I usually get three or four clues in before I give up with *The Times*."

Linus pushed his glasses up his nose and then said to Grayson, "I understand you might be interested in doing an interview with me for the paper?"

"Absolutely, if you're up for it. Ann suggested the paper broaden its scope on profiles and I'd love to get a variety of local residents to help me out and really create a good picture of Whitby."

Linus gave a decisive nod. "Then I'd be delighted to help you out."

"Great," said Grayson. "When might be a convenient time for you? My schedule is pretty flexible right now."

It appeared that Linus's schedule was also rather flexible, and I watched with a smile as Grayson and Linus retreated to one of the study tables for a talk.

The library phone rang and I picked up.

"Ann?" asked a fluffy voice on the other end.

"Hi Olivia," I said.

"Hi there, dear. I was just checking in to see if you'd made any progress on the interlibrary loans?"

Surprisingly, I had. I hadn't held out a lot of hope that there would be much available, but I'd found several titles that seemed they might be up Olivia's alley. "I took a look this morning and there are three different books, actually. Would you like me to tell you more about them?" I pulled them up on the computer.

"I'd like to check all of them out if I could. How exciting!" said Olivia.

"There's a nominal fee for interlibrary loans," I said. "Is that all right? It's $2.00 a book. It covers postage and processing."

"Absolutely fine," said Olivia. It almost sounded as if she was purring on the other end. Or maybe it was one of her many cats, perhaps draped over her shoulder.

Olivia continued, "I know you're at work now, but I'd love to tell you more about my ghostly visitors when there's a better time. You're really the only one who'll listen to me. Nate is pre-occupied with Pearl's death right now and seemed rather upset when I brought up the fact that she was spending time with me. And Justine just rolls her eyes."

I could see Justine doing just that. "Of course I'll listen, Olivia. It's a very interesting subject."

Olivia sounded pleased. "Oh good. Thanks, Ann."

Hours later, I looked at the clock. I was the one scheduled to close up, which looked like it was going to be an easy job. There were often five or six patrons still in the library near closing time but there was only one tonight and he packed up his laptop and books about twenty minutes early. I was walking around and straightening chairs, shelving recent returns, and turning off the photocopiers. I was startled to hear the library doors open.

"Hi there," I called out. "We're closing up in about fifteen minutes."

"I'm not planning on checking out any materials," said a cold voice.

Chapter Seventeen

I WALKED UP TO JOIN Justine Hill. Fitz watched warily from a distance. "Hi Justine," I said cautiously. "What can I help you with?"

Justine took a step toward me and I instinctively took a step back.

Justine said, "I've been thinking about our run-in at the park yesterday."

Run-in? It was an odd choice to describe seeing an acquaintance at a festival. I smiled tentatively at her. "Did you enjoy the festival?"

Justine waved her hand. "That's beside the point. The important thing is that you know Nate had nothing to do with his uncle's death."

I shook my head. "I wasn't thinking that he did."

I could definitely see why Nate was ready to escape his mom and move back to Georgia. She was micromanaging everything.

Her eyes were narrowed as she stared coldly at me. I felt a shiver going up my spine. Her attitude was hostile, almost threatening, as she appeared to be waiting for me to say something. I didn't. I didn't know what she wanted me to say.

She finally said, "You should be looking in another direction." She sounded almost reproachful over this.

I cleared my throat. As a matter of fact, I was. Justine was certainly starting to look like a more likely suspect. "I am, actually. After all, there are others who don't have the best alibis."

She gave me a sharp look. "So you know about that. I can't say I'm surprised. You've really been poking your nose into these murders."

I gave her a puzzled look, not sure what she was talking about. Justine didn't seem to notice, but continued on. "You obviously know his alibi was a lie."

Who's alibi? We'd just established that Nate's was. Was she talking about Samson's?

Justine still stood there as if again waiting for something. Was she waiting for me to say I wasn't going to tell Burton about Nate's murky whereabouts? Waiting for me to tell her that I trusted Nate implicitly? It was a very awkward silence. I said slowly, "Justine, if you know something, then you're in danger, too. You should go straight to Burton with that information."

Then I heard the automatic doors swish open again and Nate's voice calling out sharply, "Mom? What are you doing here?"

She spun around. "Nate? What are *you* doing here?" She turned back around to give me a suspicious look as if Nate and I had arranged some sort of late assignation at the library.

Nate said slowly, "Well, it's a library. I was going to check out some books. I just came a little late because I was held up on that job we were working on across town. I saw your car in the parking lot when I pulled in."

Justine pursed her lips. To my relief, she started briskly walking toward the exit. "I'll see you later, Nate. Goodbye, Ann."

Nate watched her go. "Okay. Well, this is one place I wasn't planning on seeing my mom. I guess I really can't escape her anywhere in this town." He gave me a curious look. "What was that all about?"

I gave a shaky laugh. "Oh, nothing really. Your mom was just looking out for you, that's all. She was concerned that you'd contradicted your alibi for your uncle's death."

Nate rolled his eyes. "Got it. Well, no matter what she says, I really don't have a good alibi for Cornelius's death. But I didn't kill him. I'm starting to think my mother believes I'm his murderer. Why else would she be so concerned about covering for me?"

I understood where he was coming from. Was she so protective of him just because he was her only child? Or was she so protective because she thought he could end up in prison if he didn't have a good alibi?

Nate said, "Anyway, enough of this. You've got to be exhausted and I know the library should be closing in the next five minutes. You'd mentioned those computer books at the festival. Do you think you could pull those out for me?"

I found the books, explained why I thought they might help him out, and then checked them out after getting him set up with a library card. After Nate left, I turned out the lights, collected Fitz, and locked the doors behind me.

The whole way home, I was thinking about Cornelius, Pearl, and the family. Cornelius's money would seem to be the biggest motive for murder, but the more I thought about it, the less sense it made to me. Justine was independently wealthy and I couldn't imagine her killing her brother for his estate. Nate could certainly have used the money, but he didn't seem to be money- focused—his only focus seemed to be getting away from his mother. And Olivia seemed perfectly content in her cottage with her cats. She wasn't even interested enough in money to acquire or hold down a job. Besides, she had an alibi.

Pearl seemed avaricious, but if she killed Cornelius, thinking Nate might benefit (and herself indirectly), then who murdered her? Samson's anger over losing his job and income could have triggered a violent response. But he seemed almost as if he was past all that—and delighted with his new job opportunity.

There was something in the back of my mind that was still bothering me, although I couldn't put my finger on it. Something that I'd just been mulling over hadn't been quite right.

I pulled into my driveway, parked, and lifted Fitz's carrier out of the car. Still deep in my own thoughts, I didn't notice anyone was around. Not until a voice said cheerily, "Hi there, Ann!"

My head whipped around. Olivia was sitting on the little bench in my front yard, hands folded, and a smile on her face.

I put my hand to my heart. "Goodness, Olivia! You startled me."

"Oh, no. Sorry, dear. I didn't mean to frighten you, especially since you were holding little Fitz there. I'm so very glad you didn't drop the dear boy." She stood up and then peered at Fitz through the bars of the carrier. "Hello, sweetie."

I had the feeling that Olivia wanted to talk about her spirit visits. I wasn't sure I was really in the right frame of mind to listen to what the apparitions of Cornelius and Pearl were doing now. She was absent-minded enough to not even have thought about the time.

I said in as cheerful a voice as I could muster, "I wish I could visit now, Olivia, but I've had a very long day at the library. I'll be working there tomorrow—do you want to pop by then? We could talk about your communications with Cornelius then, if you like. Or I could fill you in on film club or the book club and give you some flyers with our upcoming events."

Olivia blinked at me. "Is it very late?"

"I'm pretty sure nearly everyone else in town would say that it's definitely not, but I'm ready to go in, put my jammies on, and curl up with Fitz and my book." I forced a laugh. "Like I said, it was just a long day."

Olivia's eyes clouded. "Of course you do, my dear. I was just wondering if I could trouble you for a glass of water? I've been sitting here for a little while and must have lost track of time. You do have a beautiful garden."

Despite my misgivings, I couldn't really turn her away. It might be nothing. "Sure, come on in," I said reluctantly.

I unlocked the door, set Fitz's crate down on the kitchen floor, and opened it. As Olivia was cradling Fitz, I washed my hands and poured her a glass of ice water.

She took it gratefully, taking a few big gulps.

As she was drinking, though, and glancing around her with interest, I thought more about Olivia. I considered what Linus had said about Olivia keeping company with a man. I remembered Cornelius's service where Olivia and Samson had exchanged looks and I'd been pleased that at least Olivia appeared to be civil to Samson. And then I considered the fact that, as far as I could tell, Olivia had kept her relationship with whomever her beau was a secret from her family. What if Samson was Olivia's friend? And he was her only alibi for Cornelius's death.

"Goodness, but you've turned quite pale," said Olivia blithely.

She put the glass down and then gave me a sad look. "The problem is that I really like you."

"Why is that a problem?" A frisson of fear crept up my spine.

"I can't let you mess everything up. That's the problem. Justine told me that you know Samson's alibi for me was a lie."

Chapter Eighteen

I FROZE. I THOUGHT Justine had been saying that *Nate's* alibi was a lie. But she'd been really warning me about Samson. I thought she'd been threatening me, but maybe Justine had been obliquely warning me away from Olivia.

Olivia said with a sweet, sad smile, "Justine is trying to look out for me, even though she doesn't approve of me. She said family had to stick together. I know *she* won't say anything, but I don't know the same about you. In fact, Justine called me a few minutes ago and told me you'd encouraged her to go to the police with the information. I had to hurry over just as fast as I could."

I stared at her for a moment, my mind racing. I needed to keep Olivia talking if I had any hope at all of getting out of this situation. "You must miss Cornelius very much."

Olivia's face clouded. "Oh, I do, my dear. He was my beloved big brother. I have so many happy memories of us playing hide-and-seek and tag in our backyard and going to the swimming pool in the summer. It pained me so that he had to go."

"Was it because of Samson?"

Olivia said with that same, cheery smile, "See, you do know about me and Samson! That's very perceptive of you. I suppose librarians must be good at reading people, just as they're good at reading books. It's important when working with the public, isn't it? Yes, it all boiled down to Samson. But it started long ago when I was just a girl in high school. Did I ever tell you this story?"

Olivia had a faraway look in her eyes and it made me wonder if she was really altogether with me. I shook my head.

"Well, there was a boy named Parson that I was absolutely head-over-heels in love with. He was the cutest, smartest boy." She looked even dreamier now. I fumbled quietly behind me, reaching for the knife I hoped was still on my kitchen counter from this morning. Unfortunately, it looked like I'd been way too tidy and had put it in the dishwasher.

"Was he the same age as you were?"

Olivia sighed. "No, and that was part of the problem. If he had been, I think Cornelius wouldn't have had an issue with my dating him. But Parson was eight years older than me and also had had a very tough life. Despite being so brilliant, he was going to have a long road ahead of him to make anything of himself. Cornelius, who had big plans for all of us, didn't want our family to be linked to his." She shrugged. "I suppose he was a snob."

Cornelius hadn't seemed that way at all. But a twenty-something-year-old going out with someone in high school was outrageous . . . and illegal. Cornelius struck me as being very protective and I could totally understand where he might forbid Olivia to see Parson.

"What about your father?" I asked. "It seems unusual for Cornelius to have stepped into that role."

Olivia looked sad again. "He was already dead by that time. I suppose that's why Cornelius was so adamant against Parson. He was trying to protect me, but he was also treading into areas that were none of his business. That started a lifetime of Cornelius's interfering in my life."

I gingerly moved to another point on the counter in the hopes I could reach the knife block and grab one when Olivia was distracted by Fitz. Fortunately, Olivia didn't seem to mind or object to my shifting position.

"Some of the interfering was good, though, wasn't it? He helped eliminate your housing worries and helped you with vet bills." I was still stalling for time. I couldn't tell exactly where I was in relation to the knife block.

Olivia looked a little cross now. "I suppose it could be seen that way. But you have to understand how bad Cornelius made me feel about taking anything from him. He'd give me money, but his face would just be *so* sorrowful, as if he couldn't bear that I'd disappointed him again by not getting a regular job. It was quite the guilt trip."

I nodded encouragingly. "That would be really tough to swallow. You seem like a very independent person."

Olivia straightened her back a bit. "I guess I am, aren't I? I've always lived by myself, which takes an independent person. With my cats, of course." She crouched again to love on Fitz who was watching her steadily as if trying to figure something out. Maybe Fitz could sense there was something wrong, too.

As she crouched, I swiftly turned around and grabbed a knife, holding that hand behind me against the cabinets. I said in a carefully casual tone, "Was Cornelius's death something you'd planned, or something that just happened?"

Olivia's face fell. "Poor Cornelius. I'd like to say it was something that just happened because that sounds so much better, doesn't it? As if I was simply blinded by sheer frustration and lashed out. But Cornelius wasn't a stupid man. I had to try to be just as clever as he was to make his death happen."

My hand flexed around the knife. I felt much better having it in my grip. "So, I'm trying to get the big picture for how it all came together. Obviously, you and Samson started dating. I'm sort of wondering how that came about. I wouldn't have thought you and he ran in the same circles." Frankly, I didn't think Olivia ran in *any* circles.

Olivia smiled. "That's a sweet story, actually. One of my favorite cats, Howdy Doody—spotted, you see, just like freckles, had somehow slipped out of the house. The darling thing had never been out before and I didn't have any hope that he was going to be able to make his way home or even be able to survive outdoors—avoiding cars, hunting for food, avoiding bad people. I was terribly worried about him."

I said, "I think I remember your putting some posters out."

She beamed at me. "Do you? Yes, I put them all over town. Cornelius gave me a hand with it, as a matter of fact, which was very kind of him. He *could* be kind. Anyway, Samson found Howdy Doody one day—he was just sitting there right outside his front door, waiting for him. It sounds like fate, doesn't it? He brought him home to me and I was so relieved and delighted that I burst into tears. I invited Samson in for a cup of coffee and that's how it all started."

"When did you discover that Samson had something of a grudge against Cornelius?"

Olivia sighed. "That was so sad for me, as you can imagine. Cornelius behaved very badly toward Samson. I take it Cornelius didn't want to admit any fault because he was concerned about possible lawsuits and whatnot. It came out very quickly, though, to answer your question. As soon as I introduced myself, you see. Since I never married, I'm still Olivia Butler. And then Samson asked right away if I was related to Cornelius. That's when he told me the whole story."

"You must have known right away that Cornelius wouldn't accept Samson," I said softly.

She nodded briskly. "Oh goodness, yes. If Cornelius wasn't happy about Parson, he certainly wasn't going to be happy about Samson. Which broke my heart because I care so much about Samson. I tried to hide it from him for a long while. Justine still doesn't have any idea because I didn't share it with the rest of the family. But I got to the point where I didn't want to hide my relationship with Samson anymore. I wanted to share it with the world. We're so happy together. So I told Cornelius."

"And he wasn't quite as happy as you were," I said.

"Not a bit. In fact, he absolutely forbade me to see him anymore." Olivia's mouth twisted as she remembered. "I'd gone over to his new house to take the tour. He was big on taking the family around to show how great his new place was. It was at least the second time I'd seen the house under development. While I was there, I took the opportunity to tell him about Samson. Then he told me I must break up with him. He was quite vicious about it and wouldn't listen to a word I said. I told him that he couldn't tell me what to do and he said something like: 'my money, my rules.' He meant by that, of course, that since he was supporting me, he could make whatever rules he wanted to and that I needed to abide by them if I wanted his support to continue. I took that to mean I had to choose between my house and Samson."

"Did he tell you why he disapproved of Samson?"

"Not really," said Olivia. "He said it was a work-related issue and that he had reason not to trust Samson. Then I brought up that I knew how poorly he'd treated Samson after he had an injury on-site. He gave me the coldest look I've ever seen. Then he said he had work to do and I should let myself out. He walked out to look out from the deck onto the lake. It was a beautiful evening and the moon was full over the water. I was very pleased that his last bit of time in the world would be in such a lovely place on such a pretty night."

"How did you figure out how to sabotage the elevator?" I asked.

Olivia gave a tinkling laugh. "It really wasn't *sabotage*. It was a perfectly legitimate setting on the elevator. Cornelius demonstrated it to me himself. He always did like showing off how things work. And I am naturally good at mechanical things, just like Cornelius is—I just wasn't *interested* in it, like he was. Anyway, the mechanism he demonstrated holds the elevator on a particular floor. I, of course, realized that he wouldn't assume the elevator was on the bottom floor and would just step right in."

"And fall to his death," I clarified.

"That was the supposition," admitted Olivia. "And it seemed to work. So I set it up, wiped it down, and then left while he was still outside, drinking his whiskey and looking out on the water." She brightened. "You know, that's something I'd forgotten earlier. He *had* been drinking. That's probably what made him be less-cautious about entering the elevator. And, of course, there wasn't that much lighting installed in the house yet, so it was all sort of dim. I *do* feel as if Cornelius was partially at fault for his death. After all, he was the one who forced me to make a terrible decision. And he was impaired, which was entirely of his own doing."

"And Pearl?" I asked.

Olivia looked sorrowful. "That part made me a little sick, I have to admit. She was a young person and basically blameless, even if I never really warmed to the girl very much. She never tried to control my life, obviously, which was the whole entire reason I had to do away with my brother. Pearl's problem is that she was greedy."

I nodded. "She wanted you to pay up? She'd seen you at the house that night, obviously."

Olivia nodded sadly. "She said she'd been out with friends and they'd driven by Cornelius's house for a lark. Pearl had noticed my old car there. It does tend to stand out, I suppose. Anyway, she came to visit me, but it wasn't the kind of visit I wanted. She said she knew what I'd done and if I didn't want her to tell the police, I needed to pay her."

"Did she ask for much?"

"*So* much! I don't know how much money she thought I had, but she was completely mistaken. I told her I didn't have it. She said she was sure I had something I could give her until probate went through and I got Cornelius's money. Then I knew she wasn't just going to get money from me a few times and it would be done. She was talking about the money from my brother's estate and that was probably a year away."

I said, "You knew she was going to keep blackmailing you and it probably wouldn't stop."

Olivia nodded earnestly as if pleased I was following along. "And she was definitely going to tell the police if I didn't pay her. No question. In fact, I got the feeling that she was going to really enjoy telling them what I'd done. When I knew she wasn't going to stop blackmailing me, probably for the rest of my life, I realized it was just like Cornelius."

I must have looked confused because Olivia quickly added, "Because Cornelius took control of my life. Pearl was going to do the same thing. That's when I knew she had to die."

I said, "So you arranged to meet with her at Cornelius's house. Maybe you said you were going to pay her the money she'd asked for. What did you hit her over the head with?"

"Mercy, I'm not sure I remember." Her brow furrowed in thought for a few moments and then she said brightly, "There was a heavy wrench there from one of the workmen. I struck her with that and then shoved her off the deck."

I swallowed and then said, "That must have been fairly difficult. Pearl was very young."

Olivia eagerly responded, "But you see, it *wasn't* difficult at all. That's because Pearl wasn't expecting me to do anything. She thought of me as a victim, even though she knew what happened to Cornelius. She underestimated me." Her face clouded again. "What's different now is that you don't want to take control of me and my life. You're not trying to blackmail me. You've always been nice to me. But Justine said you'd figured it all out."

My throat was very dry but I managed to croak out, "How did Justine find out you had been behind the deaths?"

Olivia sighed. "Justine is just so bright and so perceptive. It's always annoyed me my whole life. You can't imagine what it was like going through school behind her. The teachers all expected this brilliant student . . . and then I'd take the first test and they'd lower their expectations. Anyway, Justine somehow discovered Samson and I were together. It was a slip of my tongue or a look . . . I'm not sure which. Then she put two and two together."

I said, still in that unfamiliar voice as I fingered the knife, "She'd been concerned that Nate was responsible for the murders. I guess she knew he didn't have an alibi."

Olivia gave that tinkling laugh again. "Nate would never have done something like that. Justine was being silly to think he would." She looked down with a serious expression at Fitz. "I want you to know that I'll take care of Fitz for you."

I acted like I didn't know what her intentions were. "That's so nice of you, Olivia. I'll be sure to take you up on that the next time I go out of town. I'm sure he'd love hanging out with the rest of your sweet kitties."

Olivia said sadly, "No, I mean after you're gone. Like I said, Ann, I don't want to have to do this, but I *must*. You'll go to Burton and tell him because you're a good citizen. I'm sure I would do the same in your shoes. And I simply can't let that happen. Samson and I are going to be together, and I have a lot to look forward to, finally, for once in my life. I just can't squander that opportunity to be happy." She picked up a cast iron skillet that she'd been eyeing earlier. "Like I said, I'll be delighted to take care of Fitz. He'll fit right in with all the other babies and will be so loved. And he even has a great name! As I recall, he was named after F. Scott Fitzgerald. A delightful name for a library cat."

Her voice was tender and contrasted drastically with the skillet she was holding. I tightly clutched the knife, needing to be closer before trying to use it. Olivia advanced toward me, a sad expression on her sweet features.

My back door flew open and a stern, grating voice said, "Ann, I saw your lights were still on."

Chapter Nineteen

OLIVIA AND I SWUNG around to see henna-haired Zelda standing there. Zelda scowled at the frying pan and Olivia. "Say, what's going on here? What's the meaning of this?"

Olivia brandished the pan at her with little jabs and Zelda snorted. "You've got to be kidding," Zelda said flatly.

Olivia gasped, dropped the pan to the floor, and shoved her way past Zelda and out the door.

Zelda narrowed her eyes at the door. "What was all that about, Ann?"

I sank into a chair around my kitchen table and laughed shakily. "I'm afraid it was exactly what it looked like. You saved the day, Zelda. And, most likely, my life."

Zelda straightened a bit. "Well, you know, sometimes I have excellent instincts." She pressed her lips together and took out her cell phone. "Police? I'd like to report a crime."

Burton was there within a couple of minutes. "Where did she go?" he asked grimly.

I shook my head. "When Zelda came in, Olivia dashed out." I paused. "If I had to guess, I'd think she might be over at Samson's place."

He nodded and rushed out again, getting on his phone as he did.

Zelda busily started making what appeared to be warm milk on my stove.

"Zelda, I'm really glad to see you. But what are you doing here?" I asked.

She opened my cabinets and frowned at the contents before finding a couple of packets of cocoa. I was relieved I wasn't just having warm milk. Zelda said, "I wanted to remind you about the porch light. It's still flickering. I decided to do some research and flickering porch lights *can* be the sign of a serious electrical defect. Plus, Prentiss is doing a sweep of the neighborhood to-morrow."

"A sweep?" I asked weakly.

Zelda nodded and whisked the cocoa into the milk in an efficient manner. "That's right. She drives around and searches for homeowner violations. I was going to tell you that you might want to spray the grass that's growing up in the cracks of your driveway. Besides fixing that porch light. But the porch light should *certainly* be the priority."

I laughed again and rubbed my face. "Zelda, I've never been so glad to have a possible homeowner association violation."

She gave me a doubtful look.

I said, "Thank you for looking after me. That was kind of you to give me a heads-up."

"What was *that* all about? That woman. Who was she?" Zelda stared ferociously at the door as if Olivia was going to pop back in at any second.

"She was Cornelius Butler's sister."

Zelda gave me a blank look and I continued, "He was a developer and builder here. He was murdered recently—you might have seen something in the paper about it."

Zelda sniffed. "I don't read the paper. And I'm very glad I don't if murders and other unpleasantries are in there."

Of course she didn't. But right now, I couldn't find any fault with Zelda at all. She was my hero for the day.

After drinking cocoa, Zelda commanded me to put my feet up on the sofa. She bustled around my small house, finding a blanket, fixing me a sandwich (after noting with some asperity the paucity of the contents of my fridge), and then pouring me a large glass of water. Then she dug up my cell phone charger and connected my phone to it. Once Fitz joined me on the sofa, Zelda finally nodded in satisfaction.

"There. Now, if you have any problems, you can call me. You'll scare me to death if you call, so make sure it's a *real* problem. Or possibly an emergency," she said grimly. "I'd have tucked you into bed except I'm assuming the police are going to want to talk to you. They'll want to talk to me, too, since I was a witness, but they'll have to come to my house to do it because I want to put my feet up, too. And perhaps have a small nightcap."

I smiled at her and said, "Thanks, Zelda."

"And I'll be back at the library very soon. An interesting place, the library."

With that, she was gone, locking the door behind her and firmly pulling it shut.

I'd let Zelda fuss over me as if I were an invalid, thinking that it was calming *her* down to get me settled. But the truth was that I was feeling very shaky and the warm blanket and the sandwich and the cat had a very lulling effect.

Burton arrived back about an hour later, tapping lightly on the door. I got up, let him in, and then retreated to my set-up on the sofa. Fitz got up to greet Burton and Burton absently reached out a hand to rub him.

"First off," said Burton, his kind eyes full of concern for me, "I wanted to let you know that Olivia is in custody."

I relaxed a little then, feeling relief run through me. "Oh, good." Then I shook my head. "Poor Olivia."

"She was mostly worried about her cats," said Burton. "But her friend Samson, who doesn't seem to be involved, offered to take them to his place. So we were able to relieve her mind about that."

I said, "Zelda, the lady who was here with me, said that she'd be a witness to what happened, but she'd need to be interviewed at her home."

Burton nodded. "Could you give me her full name and where she lives?"

I was able to provide it, although not the house number, just a description of her house and approximately where it was located on our street. Burton jotted that down in his little notebook and then called a deputy and sent him over there to take a statement.

"Now then," said Burton, leaning forward in his chair, "on to what happened here. Olivia did give a full confession, by the way. But she didn't give a lot of information as to why she decided to show up here and try to kill you. I'd like to hear some more about that if you're able to talk about it."

"I'm fine," I said. "I'm just really tired. It all started when Justine showed up at the library tonight before I left to warn me off."

Burton quirked an eyebrow. "You've had a lot of encounters with the family tonight."

"Too many encounters with them. I was already shaken when Justine showed up like that. The way she was speaking with me felt very threatening at the time. I thought she was trying to warn me away from reporting Nate and his lack of alibi to you. But according to Olivia, she was trying to tell me that Samson's alibi was no good and that I should stay away from Olivia. I was still thinking about Justine when I walked up to my house and saw Olivia."

"She was just outside waiting for you?"

"She was. And she was very pleasant the whole time. Well, you've seen her. I'm sure she was very agreeable when she was speaking with you, too," I said.

Burton chuckled. "She was, once we told her that Samson was going to take charge of her furry babies."

I said, "Olivia acted as if it really pained her to have to kill me. But she thought Justine knew she'd killed Cornelius and Pearl and that Justine was warning her. So Olivia came over to silence me." I pulled the blanket over me a bit more, appreciating the warm weight of it.

Burton said, "The way she's been determined to cover up her crime and the way she ran from here when your neighbor appeared surprised me. Why was she so focused on escaping justice? Was it just because of her cats?"

"No, although she loves those cats like they were her children. But she also wanted to spend her life with Samson."

Burton nodded. "I know she stated that she killed Cornelius because of his habit of interfering in her life. He'd told her not to see Samson anymore, from what she said."

"Exactly. She sort of blew up. That was the final straw for her. She didn't *want* to have this secret relationship with Samson, always hiding that they were together. But Cornelius was going to make that impossible."

Burton said, "Olivia did mention wanting to go public with their relationship—she was waiting until things quieted down a little and then was going to tell Justine about Samson."

"Right. So she wanted to cover up what she'd done. She murdered Pearl because she'd seen her vehicle over at Cornelius's house. And she was going to murder me because she thought Justine was telling her I knew."

Burton said, "How did your neighbor end up getting involved in all this?"

"I'm so glad she did. Burton, I had a knife in my hand and was going to have to stab Olivia in self-defense. I can only imagine how much I'd have been traumatized from doing that. Zelda came over because she's very involved in our homeowner association and she wanted to warn me that the grass growing through the cracks in my driveway was considered a violation. When Zelda came in, Olivia was reared back to hit me with the pan and I had the knife in my hand, ready to attack her. Zelda's distraction was what saved me."

Burton said, "I don't know. I'd think your knife would have been more effective than her frying pan."

"Yeah, but I wouldn't have felt like a winner. I didn't want to have to stab Olivia. In a weird way, I liked her. It's just that she didn't exactly look at the world through an appropriate lens."

"That's for sure," said Burton. He put his notebook away. "Okay, well, I think that's enough for tonight. The state police may have some follow-up questions later, but they can wait until tomorrow. You need some sleep."

He turned as if in response to a sound. Then he smiled. "Looks like you've got someone to talk things through with for a little while." His face was wistful as he stood to walk to the door.

"How are things going with Luna?" I asked softly before he could walk away.

He gave me another smile. "I think I've made some progress. Maybe."

Then Grayson was there, stooping in front of the sofa and holding my hand. He told me Zelda had called him and filled him in. We sat there quietly for a couple of minutes. I enjoyed the stillness and the feeling of being safe.

Then I said, looking up at Grayson seriously, "Hey, I'm sorry we've been playing phone tag and had all the interruptions."

Grayson shook his head. "Don't worry about that. Life happens sometimes, doesn't it?"

I hesitated. We were having such a nice moment that I didn't want to ruin things by bringing up the fact that he'd seemed distant during our last phone call. I said carefully, "It does, for sure. I just wasn't sure—well, I thought you were a little distracted the last time I tried to reach you."

Grayson reached out and gave me a hug. "I'm sorry, Ann. You're right. I was totally distracted. I had somebody in my office."

"No worries. Believe me, I totally understand."

He gave me a warm smile. "This time you probably don't *totally* understand. This particular person is a buddy of mine who owns a boat. I was in the middle of arranging a little sunset cruise for both of us for one evening this weekend. I checked on your schedule at the library before I did to make sure I wasn't going to mess anything up."

"That," I said in a heartfelt voice, "is absolutely perfect. That's awesome, Grayson."

He turned on some relaxing music from a playlist he had on his phone. And he didn't want to talk, which was so nice after the last hour. As we sat there in my living room with Fitz curled up on my lap and Grayson holding my hand quietly, I felt things couldn't get any better.

About the Author

ELIZABETH WRITES THE Southern Quilting mysteries and Memphis Barbeque mysteries for Penguin Random House and the Myrtle Clover series for Midnight Ink and independently. She blogs at ElizabethSpannCraig.com/blog, named by Writer's Digest as one of the 101 Best Websites for Writers. Elizabeth makes her home in Matthews, North Carolina, with her husband. She's the mother of two.

Sign up for Elizabeth's free newsletter to stay updated on releases:

https://bit.ly/2xZUXqO

This and That

I LOVE HEARING FROM my readers. You can find me on Facebook as Elizabeth Spann Craig Author, on Twitter as elizabethscraig, on my website at elizabethspanncraig.com, and by email at elizabethspanncraig@gmail.com.

Thanks so much for reading my book...I appreciate it. If you enjoyed the story, would you please leave a short review on the site where you purchased it? Just a few words would be great. Not only do I feel encouraged reading them, but they also help other readers discover my books. Thank you!

Did you know my books are available in print and ebook formats? Most of the Myrtle Clover series is available in audio and some of the Southern Quilting mysteries are. Find the audiobooks here.

Please follow me on BookBub for my reading recommendations and release notifications.

I'd also like to thank some folks who helped me put this book together. Thanks to my cover designer, Karri Klawiter, for her awesome covers. Thanks to my editor, Judy Beatty for her help. Thanks to beta readers Amanda Arrieta, Rebecca Wahr, and Dan Harris for all of their helpful suggestions and careful reading. Thanks to my ARC readers for helping to spread the word. Thanks, as always, to my family and readers.

Other Works by Elizabeth

MYRTLE CLOVER SERIES in Order (be sure to look for the Myrtle series in audio, ebook, and print):

Pretty is as Pretty Dies

Progressive Dinner Deadly

A Dyeing Shame

A Body in the Backyard

Death at a Drop-In

A Body at Book Club

Death Pays a Visit

A Body at Bunco

Murder on Opening Night

Cruising for Murder

Cooking is Murder

A Body in the Trunk

Cleaning is Murder

Edit to Death

Hushed Up

A Body in the Attic

Murder on the Ballot

Death of a Suitor (2021)

Southern Quilting Mysteries in Order:

Quilt or Innocence

Knot What it Seams

Quilt Trip

Shear Trouble

Tying the Knot

Patch of Trouble

Fall to Pieces

Rest in Pieces

On Pins and Needles

Fit to be Tied

Embroidering the Truth

Knot a Clue

Quilt-Ridden

Needled to Death (late 2021)

The Village Library Mysteries in Order (Debuting 2019):

Checked Out

Overdue

Borrowed Time

Hush-Hush

Where There's a Will

Frictional Characters (2022)

Memphis Barbeque Mysteries in Order (Written as Riley Adams):

Delicious and Suspicious

Finger Lickin' Dead

Hickory Smoked Homicide

Rubbed Out

And a standalone "cozy zombie" novel: Race to Refuge, written as Liz Craig